tuned in

EPISODE #6

# doggie
# dreams

## by Julia DeVillers

Printed in the United States of America

First edition

ISBN 0-9678906-0-8

Visit www.limitedtoo.com

# introduction

**This Journal Belongs to:** ☆

☆ Maddy Elizabeth Sparks ☆

Private! Keep Out!!!

OK! This is kinda cool. Here's what I'm going to be doing ...

Our principal made a speech to our school today. He said our school is going to be ...

A school that cares!

A school that helps others!

Because we are going to care and help others ...

And all students will VOLUNTEER!

I am psyched!!!!!!

OK, not everyone was psyched. Some people were like SNORE! Yawn! BO-ring. And who cares? But I think it sounds kinda cool.

The principal gave us a list of ideas. He said we could volunteer to help:

- ☐ Little kids learn to read
- ☐ Older people at a retirement home
- ☐ At a library with books
- ☐ At a hospital
- ☐ At a nature place
- ☐ At a pet shelter

<u>Guess which one I'm going to pick???!!! Help at a pet</u>
<u>shelter! I can help all the cute animals!</u>

<u>This is going to be WAY cool!!!!</u>

"This is going to be way annoying," Brittany said, hanging over the bus seat.

Brittany wasn't talking to me when she said that. She was talking to Haley and Danielle. Actually, she wasn't talking to me at all! We kinda had a fight. Not really a fight. More like she got mad at me. But I was already getting mad at her. Because lately she had been ...

Mean! Nasty! And not a good friend!

So I'd been staying away from her. She'd been staying away from me. But that was kinda hard. She's in my Choir and Wellness class. And she's Captain of the cheerleading squad. And right now I have to see Brittany because we ride the bus home together. She's sitting in front of me with Haley. They're hanging over the seat. Talking to me and Danielle.

Well, mostly to Danielle.

"Yeah," Haley echoed what Brittany had said. "Volunteering

is going to be way annoying!" She turned to Brittany. "Um, why is it going to be annoying?"

"Because," Brittany said. "I mean, puh-lease. Like I have time to volunteer? I mean, we have our first cheerleading practice this week. We will have to practice, like, all the time!"

"Well, I think volunteering is great," Danielle said. "It's great to help other people. Besides, cheerleading isn't everything."

"I'm not surprised to hear that from you," Brittany said. "It's pretty obvious you didn't put the time and energy into trying out that, shall we say, others did? Frankly, I'm surprised you even made the team again. Your jumps at tryouts? Not so great."

Danielle shlumped down in her seat.

"Hey," I whispered to her. "You made the team. Don't let her get to you."

And also ... I agreed with Danielle! I thought volunteering would be great! I felt ... good about it.

I mean ... lately ... all these great things had happened to me. I became part of the TOO Crew! I got to go on some seriously sweet trips! I even met some celebrities!

So many nice things have happened to me! I want to DO

something nice for other people!

"I think it's going to be cool," I said. "I'm going to try to volunteer at the new dog shelter."

"I'm going to help out at the library," Danielle said. "Being around all those books? That'll be great. What are you going to do, Haley?"

Haley looked at Brittany.

"What are we going to do, Brittany?" she asked.

"Oh, something way more cool than you guys, I'm sure," Brittany shrugged. "I'll get my parents to hook us up somewhere tight."

"Excellent!" Haley said.

"We also need something that doesn't take up too much time or too many days," Brittany said. "Something that doesn't interfere with cheerleading. Because you know, you guys. If you miss too many practices ..."

She made a slicing motion across her neck. Like ... CUT!

"Oh, but in your case, Maddy?" Brittany added. "Feel free to miss some practices. LOTS of them."

"But if Maddy misses lots of practices, she'd get cut from the team," Haley said to her, all confused.

"Well, we survived just fine without Maddy when she didn't make the team last time," Brittany said cheerfully. "So I'm sure we'd survive again."

ARGH!! I ignored her. Pretended to, anyway.

"Plus," Brittany turned to Haley. She talked quietly. But not too quietly. She knew I would hear her. "Then we'd get Maggie back. Since Maddy took Maggie's spot and all ..."

Maggie was this girl who didn't make the team this time. She was on it last time. I kinda felt bad about it. But I mean, I didn't steal her spot or anything! I just tried out!

"It wasn't Maggie's spot," Danielle said out loud. "And Maggie got to be on the team last time, now it's Maddy's turn. That seems pretty fair to me."

"Hmph," Brittany said. "Well, at least Jordan Cooper didn't make it again. Ha! That girl thinks she's all that! But she was soooo REJECTED!!!"

Hey! That does it. Jordan Cooper is a friend of mine. I was bummed out she didn't make it again. She was bummed, too. But Brittany didn't have to be so ...

MEAN about it!!!

Plus, Brittany knows I like Jordan. She's being nasty to bug me!!! And it's working!!!

Brittany's and Haley's heads disappeared. They slid back into their seat. They were laughing.

OK! You know what?!! I'm not going to let Brittany get away with it! I'm going to stand up to her! I'm going to tell her to stop it now!

Then I'm going to ignore her! I'm not going to talk to her. Not going to listen to her. Going to stay faaaaaaaaaaaaaaaaaaar away from her ... forever!!!

OK! I'm going to do it! I'm going to stand up for myself ...

I stood up. I opened my mouth to talk and then ...

 **SPLOT!**

Something splotted on the side of my face. Something started dripping down the side of my face. I felt it. It was green and slimy and ...

What was that????!!

"Maddy!" Danielle said. "You've been OOZED!"

I'd been oozed! I'd been slimed! Someone had thrown that

slimy ooze stuff! And it hit me!

Brittany and Haley looked up. They started to laugh! They saw me ... with green ooze dripping in my hair down my ear ... down my neck. Ick.

"Hey, Maddy!" a voice called out from the back of the bus. "Sorry! Didn't mean to ooze ya!"

It was Derek Hogan!

"HAH!" Robert's face popped up from another seat near the front of the bus. "Missed me, Hogan!"

"Yeah?" Derek yelled. "How 'bout this one!"

And then another slimy oozy thing flew right past me! Robert and Derek were throwing oozy slimy stuff at each other! Gooey! Slimy! And drippy ...

"Maddy, your hair is all green and icky!" Brittany said to me. "It looks like a runny nose all over your hair. Ewww ...!"

Argh! I sat down quick. I started to wipe my hair ... but I didn't have time! Because then I saw this girl Maya grab some Ooze. And wing it at this guy Jeff. And Jeff threw some at Caitlin! And then there was ...

**OOZE FLYING EVERYWHERE!**

OOZE FIGHT!!!!!!!

Everything was like ...

SPLAT! And AHHHHH! People were yelling when they were hit with flying ooze!

"Take cover!" Danielle said. We hid under our backpacks. Globs of wiggly jiggly ooze were flying over the seats!

And then ...

"Whoops!" I heard Robert say. And he hid under his seat.

"Oh, man!" Derek yelled out. "Robert just oozed Mumphrey!"

Mrs. Mumphrey was our bus driver. UH oh!

**SCREEEEEEEECH!!!!!!**

The bus screeched to a stop.

"WHAT is going on here!" said Mrs. Mumphrey. Coming down the aisle. With a lump of green ooze stuck to her baseball hat.

"Who threw the ooze?" she said. "Who oozed my bus?"

She looked around.

Everyone tried to look all innocent. La la la. Wasn't me. I could see Robert all scrunched in his seat. Like ... whoops!

Everyone was silent.

"Since nobody is confessing, I will enact a punishment to all," Mumphrey announced.

Robert jumped up. "Wait! It was me!"

"Too late," Mumphrey said. "I am assigning seats. From now on, you sit where I tell you. Mornings and afternoons."

She started pointing at people. Mumphrey put Abby next to Robert. Abby was all Noooooo! Don't make me sit next to him!

But Abby was stuck. Mumphrey was moving, switching, changing! And she was coming our way.

"Oh no," Danielle whispered to me. "Is she going to make us change seats?"

Mumphrey came closer ... and closer. She pointed to Haley. Made her sit next to ... who was that? I didn't even know that girl's name!

Haley was like Noooooo!!!!! Separated from Brittany!

Hee. OK, for a minute there I was smiling. 'Cuz Haley is stuck to Brittany like ... sticky ooze!!!

But I wasn't smiling for long. Mumphrey looked at our seat. She looked at me. She looked at Danielle. She pointed to Danielle and made her sit next to ... Derek Hogan. And she pointed to me. And to the seat next to ...

Brittany.

Oh no!!!!!!! I would have to sit next to Brittany? Every morning? Every afternoon we took the bus? But ... but ... but ...

Brittany didn't look too happy about it, either.

"Excuse me, Mrs. Mumphrey?" Brittany said, all sweet.

Mumphrey just looked at her.

"Would it be too much of a problem if I could have my original seatmate back?" Brittany asked. "We always work hard on our homework and study together on the bus. And by the way, your hair looks especially nice today-"

"Request denied!" Mumphrey interrupted her. She pointed to me. She pointed to the seat next to Brittany. "MOVE!" She commanded.

I moved. Next to Brittany. Ooookay. Me and Brittany. Sharing a bus seat.

Well. Maybe tomorrow we can sneak back. Mumphrey can't remember where everyone was sitting right? I won't be stuck here, right?

"And be warned," Mumphrey said. "No funny business. I know where each and everyone of you is sitting. You are to stay there. Or else ... trouble."

Or I could be stuck here.

Brittany looked at me. She took a ruler out of her backpack. She placed it on the seat between us.

"THAT is your side," Brittany said. "You stay on your side. I'll stay on mine."

AUGH!!

"And ew ... don't get ooze on me," Brittany said. "You're dripping."

AUGH!!!!!!!

# chapter 1

I walked in my front door. My brother Zack was watching TV.

He turned around and looked at me. His face was like, "Yipes!"

"I know, I have green ooze sliming down my face," I said. "There was an ooze fight on the bus."

"Man," Zack said. "An ooze fight? I can't wait til I get to ride the middle school bus. That's tight."

That kid is way warped.

"Mom made brownies," Zack said, pointing at the counter. "Want one?"

I looked at him.

"Are those really brownies? Or is that really mud in a pan?" I asked. Very suspicious.

"100% chocolatey brownies," Zack said. Then he cracked up. "But, that was pretty funny that time you ate the mud ones I made. Heh!"

I looked at the brownies close up. When you have a brother

like Zack, you have to check everything closely.

Zack reached past me and grabbed a brownie.

"Mom made the brownies for me! To celebrate!" he said, stuffing an entire brownie into his mouth.

"What'd you do?" I asked him.

"Check this baby out!" Zack said, pointing to the fridge. A certificate was hanging there:

> **Good Citizenship Award Presented to:**
> **Zachary Sparks**
> **in Ms. Weingarten's Class**

"YOU?" I was like ... Zack?! You mean Mr. Kid who is always in trouble for playing jokes on people and talking in class and not following directions and all that stuff!? "YOU got a Good Citizenship Award?"

"Yuppo," Zack said. "Ms. Weingarten told Mom I didn't get in trouble for a whole week!"

"Well, congratulations," I said, grabbing a brownie. "I think."

Mm. Good brownies.

Zack pointed at the TV.

"Hey! *Dog Stars* is on," Zack said. "Check out that dog."

This black Labrador was getting on a scooter. It started to ride! The dog was riding a scooter!!!

"Check that out," Zack said. "It's popping a wheelie!"

The judges were all like yay! They gave the dog a good score.

The next dog was a little Pomeranian. The owner said she could do math! The owner asked, "What's two plus two?"

And the dog went, "Arf! Arf! Arf! Arf!"

She got it right! Go doggie!

"I wish I had that dog," Zack said. "It could help me with my math homework."

Me too! Actually, I wish I had ANY dog. Because I LOVE dogs! But ask me if I have a dog. Noooo. Ask me if I want a dog. Yes! Ask my brother Zack. He'd say yes! Ask my Mom. She'd say yes! Ask my Dad? He'd say No! So I'm working on him.

"Zack!" my Mom yelled. "Did you finish your homework? No TV before homework is finished!"

"Yipes!" said Zack. "Busted!" He turned off the TV.

I finished my brownie. I went upstairs to say hi to my Mom. And to wash the ooze out of my hair. Off my face. And out of my ears. Ick!

```
From: Dani55
Send to: MaddyBlue

FW: Cheer Practice

Hey I noticed u were left off this e-mail list!
So I'm forwarding this to you! Luv ya Danielle


***FORWARD***
From: BrittanyCheer
Send to: Haleygrl, Dani55, Amandapanda, Shanastar,
Jadarox, ChelCB, Surya919, CareBear143, QuinnQT

Girlies! Don't 4get! 1st practice is Thursday!
Practice starts right after 7th period. Late bus,
cheerleaders! And then Saturday at 11! CU There!!!
Britty
```

Grrr! When I wasn't on the cheerleading team, Brittany would always send me e-mails about what they were doing. By "accident" she always said. Now I'm on the team ... and she leaves me out!!! I bet that wasn't an accident.

After I checked my e-mail I went to my bedroom.

SQUER SQUER! SQUER SQUER!

My guinea pig, Sugar, was saying hi to me! I went over to her cage and picked her up.

"Hi little Sugar," I said, flopping on the bed with her. I petted her soft fur. She was all PPPrt! PPPrt! Little happy noises.

I wish I was feeling happy! But I was feeling kinda bummed! This whole Brittany thing? Blugh. I didn't want to deal with it! I thought I could just stay away from her! But nooooo. Now I even have to be squished next to her every day on the bus.

How could I survive?!?! Mumphrey wouldn't let us have headphones. That way if she wanted to yell at us we could hear her, I guess. I needed a plan. I got my backpack and started filling it up with ...

Things to do on the bus (so I don't have to talk to Brittany):

⭐ Put on lip gloss (grape/raspbery combo in outside pocket)!
⭐ Think about dogs (attach dog head keychain: brown and white with big brown nose)!
⭐ Chew gum (pink bubble gum, inside pocket)!
⭐ Play with my neopet (my cute little green guy)!
⭐ Write (little notebook with my set of teeny little gel pens)!
⭐ Read my new book (it's so funny it will cheer me up)!

The phone rang.

"Maddy!" my Mom called out. "It's for you! It's Lauren!"

Lauren! From Limited Too Headquarters! Lauren was the person who invited me to be part of the TOO Crew! When she called, it always meant something ... awesome!!!

"Hi Maddy!" Lauren said. "I'm hoping you could help us out with something."

Yes! Of course! Oh yeah!

"We could use some extra fit models," Lauren said. "Your Mom said it was OK for you to come to headquarters. You come in first to be measured. Then you come back for the fittings. I'm inviting the rest of the TOO Crew as well."

"Um, what's a fit model?" I asked.

"A Limited Too fit model is a girl who tries on clothes to help them see if they fit right and look right for girls like you," Lauren said.

COOL! I think ... except ...

Me? A fit model?

"Um, but I guess I have to say this," I said. I mean, Lauren knew me! She knew what I looked like! And well, I don't have a supermodel body if you know what I mean!

"I don't think I'm exactly the fit model type," I said.

"We're not looking for supermodels, Maddy. Our fit models are real girls, like you!"

Oh. OK!! Yeess!

# chapter 2

## Dog Shelter Volunteer

Yes! That's the badge they mailed me! And I'm wearing it now! Because I'm walking into the Dog Shelter with my Mom. I was a little ... nervous! Because this was my first time volunteering. Which is kinda like a real job. I wanted to do a good job! I wanted to help all the cute little doggies!!!!

Some bells on the front door jingled, announcing that we were here!!!

"Hi!" this lady came out. "Hey, I like your shirt!"

"Thanks!" I said. I'd picked it out just for the dog shelter! I had a red and blue stripy long-sleeve t-shirt with a cartoon dog on it. I wore jeans with a red belt. And my blue Reeboks. "I'm here to volunteer."

"You must be Maddy," she said. "I'm Eve."

"I'm Maddy's mother," my Mom said.

"We're happy to have Maddy here," Eve told her. "Since we've only been open for a month, we're so pleased to have extra help."

Mom said she'd come back in an hour. Eve showed me around.

"This is the front desk where we greet people," Eve said. "Some people come in just to look around. Others want to adopt a dog that same day."

We walked around. I saw people working in each area:

- ☆ Grooming area (where the dogs are washed and fluffed)!
- ☆ Medical area (where a vet helps the dogs stay healthy)!
- ☆ The office (where all the paperwork is done)!
- ☆ The running pens (where the dogs can exercise and go for runs outside)!

And ... the kennels!

"Here's where we keep the dogs!" Eve said.

I heard all kinds of doggie noises.

"Arf! Woof! Howoooo!"

There were a bunch of cages lining the wall. Dogs everywhere!

Big dogs! Little dogs! Medium dogs! Black, white, brown, reddish, and tan dogs!

"Wow!" I said. "You have a lot of dogs!"

"Yes," Eve said. "We have even more than we expected! You'll get to know the dogs while you're here. We have some wonderful dogs."

"What kinds of things will you want me to do?" I asked.

"Most of our volunteers are older," Eve said. "Older volunteers might:

- ★ Help in the office with paperwork.
- ★ Help people find a pet to adopt.
- ★ Give tours.
- ★ Check in new dogs.

"I'll do what you need me to do!" I said.

Eve smiled. "I like your attitude. Because of your age, there are certain limits to what you can do. But you can help us in different ways, such as:

- ★ Take dogs on walks.
- ★ Clean cages.
- ★ Teach dogs commands.
- ★ Groom dogs.
- ★ Play with the dogs.

SWEET!

Well, except for the cage cleaning part. But hey.

"Today, I thought you could start playing with the dogs. It's so nice outside, the dogs will be very happy to get some fresh air and exercise. I'll stay with you today, so you get used to things."

We walked over to one of the cages. There was a tall, long-haired dog standing in it.

"This is Ginger," Eve said. "She's a mix, mostly Afghan hound. She's a real sweetheart. Very gentle. A good dog for your first day."

I held out my hand to Ginger. She sniffed it.

Sniff! Sniff! She sniffed my hand. Then she licked it. Awww! She was so sweet!

Eve put Ginger on a leash and we walked to the back door. All the other dogs were like ... Ruff! Ruff! Take meeeeee!

"Don't worry," Eve said. "They'll all get to go out and play, too."

"Do you name the animals or do they come with them?" I asked.

"Both," Eve said. "Ginger was brought in by her owner who

couldn't care for her anymore. She was already named. We name the new puppies and dogs that are brought in whose names we don't know."

We brought Ginger outside.

"Ginger isn't big into chasing balls or playing with toys. So I usually just walk her around the yard," Eve said.

"Wow! You know a lot about the dogs!" I said.

"We get to know each dog's personality well," said Eve. "Some dogs will be here for awhile. Others are adopted very quickly."

She gave me Ginger's leash. I walked around and Ginger followed.

"Good girl," I told her. I stopped and petted her. I walked around the yard for awhile.

"She really enjoyed that, Maddy," Eve said. "We can bring her in. And go get our next dog."

We went inside. All the doggies were like, Pick me! Pick me! Eve opened one of the cages and brought out a black and brown little dog.

"This is Rocky! He's a terrier. He's got a different personality than Ginger's," Eve said.

Oh yeah! I could see that!

Rocky was ...

Jumping! Bouncing! Barking! "Arf! Arf! Arf!"

"Rocky loves his outside visits!" Eve said. We took him out back. "Ginger likes to be on a leash. But Rocky likes to be let loose!"

Good thing there was a fence! 'Cuz Rocky was ... way crazy! I chased him around the yard. Bounce! Jump! "Arf! Arf!"

"Rocky will need a home where he has lots of room to play," Eve said.

I watched Rocky run and then he jumped! Right over a bench.

"Pick up a hula hoop and see what happens," Eve said. I did and Rocky jumped right through it! I held it up higher and ... Jump! He made it through!

"Wow! You go, Rocky!" I said. That dog could jump!!!

This was fun! The next dog we took out was a little black poodle looking dog. Her name was Cutie. And she was sooooo cute!

I tossed a ball around to Cutie. Aw, I loved playing with her. She jumped all over the ball. Then she jumped all over me!

I was CRACKING UP!

"Cutie will be ready for adoption tomorrow," Eve said. "She will be going home with a family who has signed up for her."

"Oh!" I said. "That's great for Cutie! But, she's so cute! I'm going to miss her already."

"I feel that way, too," Eve said. "It's easy to get attached to the dogs! We all have our favorites. But of course we're thrilled to see them go to good homes."

We brought Cutie back inside.

"Bye, Cutie," I said. "Have fun with your new family!" Cutie was all "Arf! Arf!"

The next dog was big! A tall black and brown Doberman Pinscher. Named Max.

"Um, is he friendly?" I asked. I mean, that dog was ginormous!

"Yes," Eve said. "You'll only work with dogs who are comfortable with people. We do have some other dogs who have difficulty with people or adjusting."

Eve took the big huge dog out of its cage. It came over to me.

Oooo-K! It was big and mean looking. I held out my hand for it to sniff and ... ACK!!!

Max licked me!!! Hee.

"Awww, you're a sweet doggie," I said. I patted his back.

The front door jingled.

"Oh, I guess that's your Mom," Eve said. "It's time for you to go."

Already?!!!

"I feel like I just got here!" I said. "That was way fun!"

"Time flies when you're having fun," Eve said.

I didn't even want to go! It was too fun! Playing with all those
doggies! Ginger! Rocky! Cutie! Max! But wait ...

I mean, I had fun! But I was here to help! Did I do a good job?
Did they like me?!?!

"Um," I said. "Was I ... er ... um ... do you want me to come back?"

"Definitely!" Eve said. "You were very helpful for your first
time. You were great with the dogs. We'd love to have you back.
If you want to ..."

YES!!!!!!!!!!

# chapter 3

That's my visitor's badge at Limited Too. I was at Limited Too Headquarters. The receptionist told me that fit modeling was upstairs in the Tech Design department. I went upstairs and saw Claire.

"Maddy!" Claire came over and gave me a hug. "Hi!"

"I got here early. I'm already finished!" Claire said.

"What did they do?" I asked her.

"They just measured me," Claire said. "It only took a few minutes. What's new? Did you start cheerleading yet?"

Claire and the TOO Crew had come to watch me at tryouts! They cheered me on!

"Not yet," I said. "I'm way psyched for first practice! But I did start something else. I volunteered at a dog shelter yesterday."

"Oooh, fun!" Claire said.

"Yup," I said. "Yesterday I just played with some cute dogs. But I know I'll be doing other stuff. Like helping clean cages."

"I wish I could do that," Claire said. "I love dogs." Claire has two dogs. Their names are Caesar and Duke.

"Really?" I said. "You should call the shelter. I think you could probably do it, too!"

"Oh, I don't want to budge in or anything," Claire said.

"No it would be so cool if you did it!" I said. "I'm there six times. So far on Tuesday and Friday."

"I have ballet on Fridays. And horseback riding and violin on Saturdays. But Tuesdays are free!"

"Call the dog shelter!" I said. "Ask for Eve! Tell her you're my friend."

Just then, we heard "Maddy! Claire!"

It was Kacey! Isabel! We were all like Hiiiiiiiiii!

"I'm a little late," Kacey said. "I had soccer practice." She was still in her black and gold soccer uniform.

Isabel looked totally stylin as usual. She was wearing a kinda mod black and pink shirt with a black skirt.

"Guess what," Claire said. "Maddy's volunteering at a dog shelter."

"That's perfect for you, Maddy," Isabel said. "You're such a dog lover! You have to come over and see Beans sometime." Beans is her basset hound.

"Do you get to be with the dogs?" Kacey asked.

I nodded. I thought of playing with all those dogs! Soooo fun!

"Claire's going to do it with me," I said. "You guys could, too."

"I wish I could," Isabel said. "I've already got cheerleading and jazz. My parents let me take two things. Maybe when cheerleading's over, though. I volunteered this summer teaching little kids to read. It was great."

"I'm booked," Kacey said. "Soccer! Gymnastics! Fencing! My parents let me drop violin lessons and just do orchestra in school. Yeeeeees!"

Kacey was all dancing around all happy. Because Kacey hated violin lessons! But Claire loved them! I never tried violin. But ...

I start taking piano lessons in a couple weeks. A teacher will come to my house to teach me and then Zack. Mom's idea.

Wish me luck. Because ... I'm way not musical.
You should hear me sing in Choir. Wlak! Croak!

"I'm going to be way busier soon," said Kacey. "I'll be doing my share of helping out. Because I'm going to be helping with the new baby! When it gets here!"

Kacey's Mom is going to have a baby! Kacey has a younger sister named Emily. And she'll have a new sister or brother soon!!!

Just then a woman came out and said, "Maddy? Fit room #2, please."

So I went in. I was in a room with a woman with a tape measure. All I had to do was stand there as the woman took out a measuring tape. She measured how I'd fit into pants and shirts and stuff.

"That'll do it," the woman said. "Thanks."

That was easy! Even I couldn't screw that up!

I walked back out where everyone was.

Kacey, Isabel, and Claire were walking around looking at clothes hanging on the walls.

"Look at the lines on these pants," Isabel said. "I like how they flare a little here but they're looser here."

"They're a pretty color," Claire said.

"Feel the fabric," Isabel said. "Look at the trim. A good choice."

"You really know a lot about fashion," I said to Isabel. Isabel wants to be a fashion designer someday. You can practically tell just looking at her! She always looks so together! And she makes some of her clothes and her accessories.

"I've got a lot to learn!" Isabel said. "But I love it."

"That's so cool!" Kacey said.

"What do you want to be someday?" I asked Kacey.

"I don't know yet!" Kacey said, bouncing all over the place. "But maybe I can go pro in soccer! Or basketball! Or be a sportscaster! I might want to be a pediatrician. Or an orthodontist like my Dad. Or a chef. Or something in computers. Or an actress. Or a pop star!"

Kacey did a little dance move. We were cracking up!!!

"How about you, Claire?" Isabel asked.

"Maybe a teacher," Claire said. "Or a journalist."

---

**Maddy's list of what she wants to be someday**

✓ Vet
✓ Actress
✓ Author
✓ Mom
✓ Photographer

---

"Hi girls!" Lauren walked in the room. "Hope everything is going well?"

"We all just got measured," Kacey told her.

"I love being in this room!" Isabel said. "It so makes me psyched to work in fashion someday."

"Glad to be inspiring you," Lauren said.

"Isabel will be a great fashion designer!" I said. "I bet she could practically do it now!"

"Hey, I've got a long ways to go!" Isabel said. "I'm going to take an illustration class when cheerleading ends. So I can sketch the designs I come up with. I'm going to take a junior businessperson class so I can learn more about business stuff. I'm saving up for a better sewing machine, too."

Wow!

"I'm impressed, Isabel," Lauren said. "You recognize there's a lot that goes behind the scenes when it comes to clothing. I'm glad to see your enthusiasm. You'll be particularly excited about your next assignment, Isabel."

"What?" Isabel asked.

"I can't tell you yet," Lauren said. "But I think you're all going to enjoy it! And as a thanks for your help today, help yourself to an item from this basket."

She held out a huge basket. Necklaces! Bracelets! And rings! Woo hoo! Sparkly! Shiny! Funky! Which should I choose?

Kacey picked a sporty wristband with a watch in it!

Isabel picked a choker with brown and black beads in it!

Claire picked a silver ring with two hearts on it!

And I picked a necklace that had a dangly dog charm on it!!! Perfect!!!!

"Look, Maddy got a dog on hers!" Kacey said. "A cute little poochie!"

"Perfect!" Isabel said. "You know where you'll have to wear

that! When you do your school project, Project Pooch!"

We all cracked up! **PROJECT POOCH !!!!!!**

So why am I writing on the back of my practice math quiz? Instead of my journal? Because I decided not to bring my journal to school anymore! 2 reasons! #1 - What if I lose it and someone reads it! #2 - What if Brittany takes it and reads it out loud!!!!

She did that to Chelsea B. that one time! She read her journal to everyone! So I'm taking noooo chances.

Brittany! Making me way cra-zy! When she got on the bus this morning she was all like, "Maddy? You're sitting in my spot."

I was like, what spot? I'm sitting in the seat we got assigned. Then she goes: "The window is mine."

Why does she get the window seat? Ugh. But I moved over. Not worth it.

So Brittany sat down and pulled out that ruler. She puts the ruler down the middle again. Like MY territory here. Maddy's territory there. Her territory was bigger.

I can't wait to get off this bus!!!

## PROJECT POOCH Day 2

I walked into the dog shelter. I was excited to see Rocky! And Ginger! And Max! And all the other cute little doggies!!!!

"Hi Maddy!" Eve came to the front of the room. "Thanks for telling your friend Claire about us. She's going to start volunteering on Tuesday."

Cool! We walked back to the dog area.

"Today's job is going to be down and dirty," Eve said. "We were a little busy today and didn't get to clean all the cages this morning. It's so important for the dogs to feel comfortable. And to keep them healthy. Do you think you're up for helping me with that?"

OK! Not as much fun as playing with the dogs. But I thought about all those dogs. In yucky cages. Poor doggies! I wanted to help.

"Yes!" I told her. "I have to clean my guinea pig's cage."

And Sugar gets stinky! Seriously stinky! Like PU bad! So ... I can do this!

The first cage we had to clean was for a chocolate lab named Theo. First we took out his blanket and his dog bowls. Then we had to clean up ...

Um ...

The messy parts. You know what I mean.

Sweeping! Washing! It was hard work! I thought about playing with the dogs the other day. That didn't even seem like work! This did.

"Good work, Maddy," Eve said. "Let me bring Theo back in now."

She went and got Theo. He walked into the cage. He sniffed around. He lay down in his fresh blanket. And was all ...

SIGH!

"I think he likes it!" I said. "I think Theo is happy he has a clean cage!" All of a sudden I was feeling good about cleaning his cage! Let's do the next one!

The next cage was for a Dalmatian. She was all black and white polka dots and her name was Dotti! Her cage took like two minutes to clean.

"Dotti is a very neat dog," I said.

"Yes, Dotti's cage is always easy to clean," Eve said. "She will be a good dog for someone who likes their dogs on the neater side."

Dotti licked my hand when she came back in her cage!

"I think she's saying, thanks!" I told Eve.

"I think so, too!" Eve said.

We walked over to the next cage. It was empty. The sign on the cage said "ZAK."

"His name is Zak?" I said. "That's funny! My brother's name is Zack. With a C."

"This Zak was brought in to us last week," Eve said. "He's,

well, quite a character. He must be out in the dog run."

Oh! Wow! Zak's cage was ... messy. Seriously way out of control messy.

"Wow, he's SO like my brother," I said. "You should see my brother's room! Disaster area!"

I started sweeping up pieces of food.

"I don't think he eats his food," I said. "I think he just throws it everywhere."

Then I noticed pieces of blanket everywhere! And pieces of dog chew toys!

I guess he doesn't eat his food 'cuz he's already full! From eating his blanket and toys!

It took us way longer to clean Zak's cage than Dotti's. We swept! And scrubbed! And cleaned! And then I laid out a new blanket on a dog bed. All nice. And filled his dog bowl and water dish.

Tada!

"It looks great," said Eve. "Oh, here's Zak now."

I heard a noise. It was like ... — ZWAK!!!

A big sneeze and a snort all together! I turned around and OH!

That must be Zak. He was round and brown with wrinkles. He had chubby short little legs. And had one tooth sticking out like a fang.

"Whoa," I said. "What kind of dog is he?"

"He's part bulldog," the guy holding his leash said. "The rest of him ... we're not so sure."

ZWAK! ZWAK!

"His snorts sounded a little like the name Zak," Eve explained. "He came in without a name so that's what we call him."

ZWAK! And then the dog went ... AH-SNEEZE! Zak sneezed! And gobs of greenish goo were flying and ... OK, no details! It was pretty ... gross!

It looked like the ooze fight from the bus!

"Towel!" called the guy. Eve ran and got a towel to wipe off the dog's face. The dog went, "Snortle, snortle."

"Let's put him in his cage," Eve said.

"Look, Zak," I said. Staying far away. You know. In case he

sneezed again. "Your cage is all clean!"

Zak waddled into his cage. He went Zwak! Zwak! He went over to his blanket. And started rolling around in it! Attacking it! Biting it into pieces! He pushed his nose into his dog bowl and sneezed! Dog food went everywhere!

"I told you that dog is a character," Eve said. "He really is a sweetie, but he has a unique personality."

Zak looked at us. And burped.

"As I was saying," Eve laughed. "Very unique."

OK! I like dogs and all! But that dog ... is way crazy!!!

"Um, bye Zak," I said, when I left the cage. Zak looked at me and went, "Snort!"

Oooo-K! Moving on! I kinda was hoping the next cage would be cleaner. We went to the next cage. Yes. It was neater.

And oh! There were a bunch of little puppies in it! Four puppies snuggling in a bed! Soooo cuuuuuuute!

"These are Sunny, Sammy, Sparkle, and Stacy," Eve said. "They're our newest puppies. They're ready for adoption today."

"They're so sweet!" I said. The one woke up. She came over and pushed her head on my leg.

"That's Stacy," Eve said.

We heard the noise of a bell.

"That's the front door," Eve said. "Someone's here. I'm not sure if anyone's out front so let me go check."

"Do you want me to come with you?" I asked.

"You've been working so hard," Eve said. "Why don't you take a break and play with the puppies.

The other puppies were waking up! They were cute little fuzzballs! One climbed on my lap. Another started chewing on my hair! I was snuggling! And petting! And playing with puppies!

Eve walked back with a girl with brown hair and her parents. They were looking in all the cages. Then the girl walked over where I was with the puppies. She was like, "Awwwwww!"

"Maddy," Eve said to me. "It's almost time for your Mom to come. Why don't you go wash up after all that hard work."

I washed up and headed to the lobby. Then I saw the girl with brown hair holding one of the puppies. It was Stacy! Her parents were signing some papers. She must be adopting Stacy!

That's so cool! She's getting a dog! She's so LUCKY!!!!!!!!!

This morning I told Dad that I was volunteering at the dog shelter. Like, la la look how responsible I am with dogs!

Dad said, "That's great! Volunteering not only helps others. It helps you build good character and become a better person."

"I'm going to learn a lot about dogs!" I told him. "I'll know all about taking care of dogs! I'll be a dog expert!" HINT! HINT!

But Dad just goes, "Have a good time."

So. No dog today. But I'm not giving up!!!!!!!!

The brown-haired girl was snuggling Stacy. Stacy was licking her nose! Aw! The girl walked out with her parents. And a new puppy!

Eve came over.

"That's the best part of my job," Eve said. "When we find the right loving home for one of the dogs."

NICE!

# chapter 4

Private Chat Room: PomPomCheer!

Entering chat room: MaddyBlue
Participants: BrittanyCheer, Haleygrl, Dani55,
Amandapanda, Shanastar, ChelCB, Surya919,
CareBear143, QuinnQT

AmandaPanda: Hi Maddy!

MaddyBlue: Hi guys!

Brittanycheer: We're waiting for Jada. Every1
else is here. Haley, Danielle, Amanda, Shana,
Chelsea, Surya, Caroline, and Quinn

Dani55: Maddy how wuz the dog shelter?

MaddyBlue: So many cute puppies!

QuinnQT: 2 kewl!

MaddyBlue: I had 2 clean cages 2day tho! Kinda
stinky!

BrittanyCheer: EWWW. I can't believe u would do
that.

Haleygrl: Yeah gross. Me and Britt wouldn't do
that.

Surya919: What r u guys doing for volunteering?

```
BrittanyCheer: We gave $ to some charity.

Amandapanda: How did u make the $? Fundraising?

BrittanyCheer: No. My Dad just wrote a check. Way
better than picking up dog doo doo like Maddy.
Ick!

Haleygrl: So gross!

Entering Chat Room: JadaRox

AmandaPanda: Hi Jada! k! Every1s here. We need 2
talk about the Bake Sale ...
```

Everyone was chatting about the bake sale. It was hard to concentrate. I was not happy about Brittany's comments. OK, cleaning dog cages? Not way glam. But having your father write a check for your volunteer project?

Not very ... volunteery! I felt good about helping the doggies! Even if it meant hard work!

Dling-dling!

My bedroom doorbell! Mom got me a doorbell shaped like a puppy. She thought Zack would ring it! Instead of busting in on me!

Dling-dling!

It must be Mom or Dad. I opened the door. But, nope! It was Zack.

I shut it quick.

"Why are you ringing my doorbell?" I called through the door.

Zack never used the doorbell. He still tried to bust in. Or bang on the door. Way loud. Anything but the doorbell. To make me crazy.

"Dinnertime! Dad made his famous Spaghetti ala Sparks," Zack said.

Yum!

"He made it my favorite way," Zack said. "With extra gigundo meatballs. To celebrate."

"What are we celebrating now?" I asked.

"This!" Zack said. "Check these babies out."

I peeked through the door. Zack had stickers on his forehead. I looked closer.

"Whose are those?" I asked.

"Mine!" Zack said. "From school. My teacher gave them to me."

"On purpose?" I asked. Zack's stickers usually said: "Try again!" or "See me!" or "Parent conference needed."

"Yup! They're mine. For my homework this week," Zack said. "Now hurry up, dude. Spaghetti ala Sparks is gonna get all cold and mushy."

First a good citizenship certificate. Then good work stickers? Very suspicious. Hm?!

# chapter 5

**PROJECT POOCH Day 3**

I walked into the dog shelter. Volunteering ... Day 3! I was excited! To volunteer. And also because it was Volunteering Day 1 ... for Claire!

Claire was already in the lobby talking with Eve. Claire looked ready to be with the dogs. She was in jeans and a long-sleeved pink t-shirt. And sneakers. Her hair was up in a ponytail.

"Wow!" I said. "You're usually in a skirt or dress or something."

"Well, I thought we might get messy," Claire said. "Cleaning cages and things."

Claire didn't look like the kind of person who cleaned anything! She was so pretty. Way glamorous looking. And always so neat and stuff.

"Glad to hear you don't mind a little dirty work," Eve said.

"Oh, I muck my horse's horse stalls," Claire shrugged. "I'm used to it."

Claire has a horse! Named Skydancer.

"Well, no mucking today," Eve said. "We'll break you in easy, Claire. I thought you girls could take the dogs to the exercise yards. Just like Maddy did her first day."

Cool!

"Maddy, you're so good with the dogs," Eve said. "You'll be a good teacher for Claire."

I'm good with the dogs! That's what she said!!!!

"We'll start off with a playful dog," Eve said, opening one of the cages. It was a Golden Retriever. The sign said Jake. He was really jumpy!

Jake was sooo excited to go outside! He ran right over to a frisbee. He picked it up and brought it over.

"Want to play frisbee?" I asked him. OK! I threw the frisbee to him.

"Good boy," I said. I gave it to Claire to toss next.

"He's such a cute dog," Claire said. "I wish I could adopt all of them!"

"I know," I agreed. "That's what I keep thinking. But you're lucky. You have two dogs. And even a horse!"

"Yes," Claire said. "Caesar and Duke are good dogs. And I love having Skydancer. I wish you could see her. She's so beautiful."

"I've never ridden a horse," I said. "I mean, pony rides at the fair. But that's all."

"Really?" Claire asked. I threw the frisbee to Jake. He chased after it. "Do you want come over to my house after we're done here? You could see Skydancer."

"I don't know," I said. "It's a school night. But we could call my Mom and ask."

Claire reached into her coat pocket. She pulled out her cell phone.

"Call her," she said. "I have tons of free minutes. Take your time."

"Don't you have to ask?" I said. Claire lived with her father.

"Oh," Claire said. "I guess so. My Dad is on a business trip. But I could ask Bruno or Dee. Dee used to be my nanny when I was little. But she stays with us overnight when my Dad's out of town."

I dialed home. I asked my Mom.

"Um, my Mom wants to talk to you," I said. "She has some

questions."

I heard Claire go, "Bruno will be home and the housekeeper ... Bruno can drive her home ... Dee will make us dinner ... Home by 7:30 is fine."

Claire hung up. "She said she's calling Bruno to make sure it's OK."

Bruno is this guy who works for Claire's father. He drives her around. He went on some trips with us and the TOO Crew. So my Mom knows him.

We played fetch with Jake for a few more minutes. He was really good at catching the frisbee! He caught every one!

Then Claire's cell phone rang.

"It's Bruno," Claire said. "Your Mom said yes!"

YEAH!

I'd never been to Claire's house before! FUN!

I threw the frisbee to Jake. But whoops! Bad throw! Too much to the left! And right into ...

OOF!

Eve's stomach.

"Ulp!" said Eve.

Ohmigosh! Whoops! "SORRY!" I said.

"I'm all right," said Eve.

> **Red-face Rating:** ★★★ out of ★★★★★ stars.
> *Ack! I just frisbeed the Boss!!!*

"OK, got my breath back," Eve said. "Looks like Jake has enjoyed the frisbee session. Let's go get another dog to bring out," she said. "Maddy can practice her frisbee aim."

We went in with Eve to get another dog. Hey! There was Ginger! I stopped at her cage to say hi. I waved to Dotti. And Theo. I didn't see Rocky. Then I went to see the puppies. I knew Stacy was gone and it looked like Sunny was, too! I waved to Sammy and Sparkle.

"Maddy, did we lose you?" Eve called down the hall.

"Sorry! I was just saying hi to the dogs!" I said. Then I heard a noise.

ZWAK! ZWAK!

It was Zak the Dog! Um. I'd say hi to him later! I hurried to catch up with Eve and Claire.

"Where's Max?" I asked Eve. Max's cage was empty.

"He was adopted by a nice man today," Eve said. "We were very happy for them."

Yay, Max!

Just then we heard the front door bell ring. And a voice called out, "Eve!"

"Looks like our volunteer at the front desk needs some assistance," Eve said. "Let's go on up."

We went into the front lobby. There was a woman standing there with a blanket in her hands. The blanket was wriggling. The woman looked upset.

"There must be a little dog in there," I whispered to Claire.

"I just found this puppy out in the street," the woman said. "She doesn't look well. Can you help her?"

The woman held up the blanket for Eve to see. But Claire and I saw, too.

It was a teeny tiny little puppy! With big huge eyes! She was all dirty! And shivery!

Achoo! The puppy sneezed. And shivered. And shook!

Ohhhhhhh!!!!!! The poor doggie!!!

"Why don't you girls go visit the dogs for a little while," Eve said to us. "So I can take care of this puppy for a bit?"

Eve asked the front desk volunteer to page the veterinarian. She took the puppy from the woman and wrapped her in a clean blanket. Claire and I walked back to the dog cages.

"That poor little dog!" I said. "It was so cold! So shivery!"

"And so tiny," Claire said. "I hope it's not sick. I hope it's OK!"

Poor doggie! That doggie just has to be OK!

She just HAS to!!!!!!!!!!!!!!!!!!!!!!!!!!

We were both quiet. We walked around, petting some of the dogs through the cages. They were all happy to see us. Bark bark! Woof woof! I was happy to see them. But I kept thinking about the little puppy.

"Oh!" Claire said looking at a cage. I looked over. It was Zak's cage.

"That's Zak. That dog is crazy," I said. I peeked in his cage. Yup! Blankets and food and stuff everywhere. Zak came to the bars of the cage and sniffed at us. Then he rolled over on his back and wriggled around.

Claire scratched his belly. "He's funny," she said.

Then Zak did one of his sneezes! Ah-Choo!

"Ack!" Claire said, jumping back. "That was ... gooey!"

Zak burped.

"Let's go visit Dotti," I said. "No sneezes. No burps!"

Eve came over when we were patting Dotti's head.

"Is the little puppy going to be OK?" I asked.

"She'll be just fine," Eve said. "The vet is cleaning her and warming her up."

YAY!!! Claire and I were all dancing around! YAY!!! She's going to be OK!!!

"I was so worried!" I said.

"I was, too!" Claire said.

"Do you want to come see her?" Eve said. "She's a friendly little thing."

We went into the room. The puppy was wrapped in a new pink blanket. She'd been washed off and was all white and fluffy. She had two black spots on her back.

Eve handed the blanket to me.

"She's so cute!" Claire said. I held her in my arms. The puppy looked up at me with her huge black eyes. She was so cuddly! So snuggly!

"Look at those big eyes," Eve said. "And she's so tiny. She looks like a little bug."

"The black spots on her back are like a ladybug's," Claire said.

"Cute little buggie," I said. "Sweet little lovebug."

"There we go," Eve said. "I'll check her in as Lovebug. We'll call her Buggie."

Buggie!

"Hi little Buggie," I said, scritching her head.

"I have to fill out a lot of paperwork," Eve said. "Health and medical reports. And see if anyone has reported her missing.

See if we can find her owners."

"What kind of dog is she?" I asked Eve.

"She looks mostly shih tzu," Eve said. "She looks like she'll stay pretty small."

Cute little teeny weeny Buggie!

Eve held out her arms and took Buggie. "She needs some rest."

"Bye, Buggie," Claire and I said.

"Ready, girls?" a voice said from behind us. Bruno! He was here to take us to Claire's house!

"See you next time," Eve said. "Thanks again for all your help."

We went out to Claire's car. Bruno held the door open for us. We climbed in the back seat. Whoa! It was all leathery and shiny and comfy.

"This car is sweet," I said. My Mom had a minivan. Not a leathery and shiny one, either! One with Zack's messy stuff all over it!

"What would you like for dinner?" Claire asked.

"Whatever you're having is fine," I told her.

"No, you can choose. We can ask Dee to make whatever we want," Claire said. "She's really nice."

"Oh, um, OK," I said. I only got to pick dinner on my birthday. "Maybe hamburgers? Mac and cheese?"

"Sure," Claire said. "My Dad's away on business all the time. So Dee pretty much lets me choose."

She's so lucky!

We pulled into a long driveway. WOW. Claire's house was ... huge! OK, I mean I know her father is some big businessman. But this house is a serious mansion!

WOOOF! WOOOF! These two German Shephards came running over. They were all sniffing me.

"Down, Caesar! Down, Duke!" Claire said. "It's OK. That's Maddy!"

I held out my hand. The dogs sniffed it. And then took off across the yard.

"They're trained as watchdogs," Claire told me. "They don't play too much."

We walked in through the garage.

"May I take your coat, please," Claire said. She took my coat.

Then ...

We just stood there. I looked around. We were in a big huge room with shiny wood floors and really tall ceilings. I looked at the artwork and statues.

"Um, do we need to tell anyone we're here?" I said.

"Dee knows. Bruno buzzed us in, remember?" Claire said.

We stood there.

"Do you want to show me your room?" I asked.

"Oh!" Claire said. "Yes!"

I followed her up a set of stairs. Then we went up another set of stairs!

"It's like you need an elevator in this place!" I said.

"Oh, did you want to take the elevator?" Claire said. "We could have done that."

Ohmigosh!

"This is my bedroom," Claire said.

It was huge. It was mostly white with some pink flowers. White furniture. Two pictures of horses were on the walls. There was a silver frame with a picture in it by her bed.

"She's pretty," I told her, looking at the picture.

"That was my Mom," Claire said. I knew Claire's Mom had died when she was little. Claire looked really sad.

"Um, what's that?" I asked pointing. Because there was a door opened to another room.

"That's the suite," Claire said. We went in. It was a whole other room for her! This one was yellow and flowery. There was a desk and bookshelves with a ton of books.

"Oooh! That's cool!" There was a bench under a window.

"That's my window seat," Claire said. "I sit there and read and write in my diary."

"Your room is awesome," I said. I mean, I liked my room! It was blue and white. I made it to look like the ocean. I put my shell collection up! And lots of pictures of my friends, too! But Claire's room ... and her suite ... WOW.

"What would you like to do?" Claire said.

"What do you usually do first with your friends?" I asked.

"Well, actually," Claire said. "You might think this is silly. But you're the first friend I've had over."

HUH???

"Your friends usually don't come over here?" I asked her.

"I kind of don't have too many friends here," Claire said. "I just started at my new school. Before that I had a tutor at home ever since we moved here. I didn't meet too many people."

Oh.

"What do you usually do after school?" I asked her.

"I like to draw and I'm learning how to knit. If I don't have ballet, piano or violin, I usually ride Skydancer," Claire said. "I'm practicing for a jumping competition, now."

"Can we go see her?" I asked.

"Yes!" We walked outside. We walked across a big lawn to a fence. There was a barn. And there was a horse!!! Skydancer!

Wow. COOL. She was dark brown. And really tall. Claire went to this barrel and got out some carrots.

"Do you want to feed her?" Claire asked.

Um. OK. The horse was really pretty. But she was also really big. Big like in, SCARY BIG!

"You can do it," I said.

Claire held her hand out flat. Skydancer ate the carrots off her hand.

"She likes her nose petted," Claire said.

Oookay. I held out my hand. Then I petted her nose. It was sooooooo soft!

"Hello, Claire!" a woman came out of the barn.

"Michele, this is Maddy," Claire said politely. "Michele is my riding instructor. She takes care of Skydancer, too."

"Would you girls like to ride, today?" she asked.

Uh. Um. I looooooove animals, right? I looooove dogs and cats and guinea pigs and dolphins but ...

Claire? Looooooves horses. Some of my other friends? Looooove horses. Me? Kinda scared of them.

"Um, maybe next time?" I said.

"Anytime, just let me know," Michele said. She opened the gate and started putting a saddle on Skydancer.

"Have you ever ridden a horse, Maddy?" Claire asked.

"Well, not really," I said. "I even fell off the pony ride at a festival. I mean, I was only three, but ..."

OK! I did. I fell off. In front of all those people! I was like Whoops! Not hurt. But totally ... embarrassed!!

Chances I will ride Skydancer without falling off:

0% ☹ ——————————— 100%

"Anytime you want to try, let me know," Claire said. "Michele is a wonderful teacher. And it's so much fun! You feel so free!"

Maybe ...

I watched Michele climb up on the saddle. Oh! She started riding her! Skydancer was walking, then galloping, then running!!!

Soooooo cool!!!!

"Ohmigosh," I said. "That looks so cool." Maybe sometime ... I would try it.

But not go very fast. We walked back into the house.

"Michele seems nice," I said.

"She is! I have a lot of nice people around me," Claire said. "Like Bruno and Dee."

"Don't you want to have any other friends over?" I asked her.

Claire is pretty shy! But she's so nice! She has to make new friends!

"I was thinking, this is a good start inviting you," Claire said. "I mean, I knew I could feel comfortable having you over. You're so nice!"

AWWWWW.

"There are a couple girls at school who are nice," Claire said. "And a girl I met in horseback riding."

"You should invite one of them over," I said. "I bet they'd love to see Skydancer."

DING!

We heard this loud bell noise.

"That means dinner's ready!" Claire said. "Hamburgers and mac and cheese, just like you wanted!"

# chapter 6

**This Journal Belongs to:**

_Maddy Elizabeth Sparks_

Mr. "Good Citizen" that means YOU!!!!

I went to Claire's house! It was pretty fun. We had anything we wanted for dinner.

Nicest house I ever saw: Claire's

Nicest horse I ever saw: Claire's!

Maybe sometime I'll ride Skydancer. But not today! Too big! Too tall! And I'm too ... SuperKlutzy!!! I know I would be like ... splat!

It all looked so perfect! But ... I guess it's not.
Claire seems really lonely. She's so shy! I hope she
makes some new friends soon!

"Did you have a good time at Claire's?" my Dad asked me. I
was at the kitchen table. Doing homework. My Dad and Mom
were cleaning up the kitchen. Zack was ... being Zack.
Annoying!

"Yeah! I saw her horse. We got to have whatever we wanted
for dinner!" I said.

"Guess what?" Zack said. "I got to pick dinner, too!"

"That's right, Zack," my Mom said. "Tell Maddy why."

"Check this baby out!" Zack said. It was a note from Zack's
teacher.

Dear Mr. and Mrs. Sparks:

I wanted to let you know how much improvement I've seen in Zack's
conduct in the past few weeks. He is far less disruptive to the class
and he is completing his classwork. Please let Zack know to keep up
the good work!

Ms. Weingarten

P|es

"I asked for double cheeseburgers and pizza and steak and chicken wings and chocolate cake!" Zack said.

"He got the pizza," my Mom told me. My Mom and Dad went to the living room.

"Mm, Pizza!" Zack said.

"So Zack," I said. "What's up with all the good behavior stuff? Did Mom say she is going to have Mrs. Hubert babysit if you don't shape up?"

"Yipes!" Zack said. "Mrs. Hubert! Nope. That's not it. I just decided to turn over a new leaf."

Hm. Very suspicious. Very not Zack-ish. Hm.

The phone rang.

"Zack!" my Mom said. "It's for you. It's a ... girl?!!"

A girl?!?! A girl calling Zack?!!! Ohmigosh!

Zack picked up the phone. I tried not to listen. OK, not really. I listened and this is what happened ...

Zack was all like, "Hello? Yeah. It's Zack. Oh. Whatever. Bye."

Then he hung up. He ran over to the family room couch! He

pulled a blanket over his head!

OK! What just happened??! Girls are calling for ... Zack??!!!

"Oooooh, Zacky," I said. "Do you have a girlfriend??"

"NO!" he yelled. "No girlfriend! Be quiet!"

"Who was that calling?" I was totally teasing him. Because ...
he deserved it!

The phone rang again. I jumped up! I ran for it! I beat Mom to
it!

"Sparks residence," I said.

I heard some giggles! More girls!!

"Is Zack there?" the girl asked.

"May I ask who is calling?" I said. All polite.

"Um, Stephanie," the girl said.

Zack stuck his head over the couch. He was all shaking his
head. Like Nooo! I'm not here!!! Don't make me talk!!!

"He's not here at the moment," I said. "May I take a message?"

"Uh, ask him if he likes Kylie. OK bye."

Click! She hung up!

"Ooh, Zack!" I said. "I have a message for you! From a girrrrl."

"What is it," Zack said. All mumbly under the blanket.

"That was Stephanie. She wants to know if you like Kylie." I said. "Oooooohhhhh!"

"Yipes! Stop that," Zack said.

I went over to the couch. I sat down next to him.

"Does this have anything to do with ... all the good behavior?" I said. Ha! That explains everything! My brother is trying to impress a girl!!!!!!!!

"NO!" Zack said. "OK maybe. Now go away." This was fun! Usually my brother is torturing me! MY turn!!!!!!!

"Zack and Kylie sitting in a tree!" I sang.

"Yipes!" The blanket went back over his face.

Hee!

Zack has a crush! Hee hee hee.

# chapter 7

## PROJECT POOCH Day 4

Doggie time! I couldn't wait to see the ... puppies!!!

"Hi, Eve!" I said when she came out front. "What will I do today?! Play with the dogs? Walk them! Clean cages? I was excited to see Rocky and Dotti and the little puppies and Jake and of course ... Buggie!!!

"Hi, Maddy," Eve said.

"How's Buggie?" I asked.

"She's doing great. She's a tough little puppy. We haven't heard from any owner yet, though," Eve said. "Today, I thought we'd have you groom the dogs. I'll be bathing, you'll be brushing. How does that sound?"

Fun!

"I just finished washing a border collie mix named Fifi," Eve said. "She is very gentle. Plus she has nice long hair to brush."

Eve handed me a metal brush and a soft brush. She watched

me as I brushed Fifi.

"Woof! Woof!" Fifi said. She leaned closer to me. She liked it!

"She's really enjoying this," Eve said. "Keep it up, and I'm going to go wash the next dog."

I patted! I brushed! I petted! La la la, patting, petting, brushing. I started singing a new song I'd heard on the radio.

Fifi all of a sudden jumped up on her back legs. And started walking around on her back legs! And moving back and forth!

I stopped singing. Fifi got back down. I started singing. Fifi got back up.

?? Huh?? I called Eve in.

"OK, I'm a way bad singer," I said. "So plug your ears. But you have to see this!"

I started to sing. And yup, Fifi started to walk around on her back legs! Swaying back and forth!

"Oh my!" Eve said. "I think Fifi's dancing!"

Yes! Fifi was dancing!!!!! Eve started singing with me and Fifi was dancing ... definitely dancing around!

"Maddy, you've uncovered Fifi's secret talent!" Eve said. "Fifi dances!"

How cute was THAT?! Eve gave Fifi a doggie treat!!!

"And by the way, her fur looks great!" Eve said. "Good job. I'll go bring out the next dog."

Then she went to bring the next dog out. I hoped it would be Ginger! Or Rocky! Or Jake! Or maybe Sparkle or Sunny, those cute little puppies!

Next up was ...

ZWAK! ZWAK!

Oh! I could hear him coming down the hall. It was that Zak dog! That messy, snorty, sneezy dog.

OK. The ZWAK noise was coming closer! Oooh boy.

Eve brought Zak into the room. He didn't have much fur. But what he did have was sticking all up! Spiking and poking out! He would be a serious challenge for Maddy's Dog Grooming.

"OK, Maddy, time to make Zak all pretty," Eve said. Zak went Ah-SNEEZE! Eve wiped the goo off her pants. "Well, maybe that's not the best way to put it. Time to brush Zak!"

She handed me his leash. Zak came over. All wheezy! And sneezy!

"Hi, Zak," I said. "OK. I'm going to brush you."

Zak looked at me and went ZWAK!

I took the brush. I put it on his head.

Zak started wriggling.

"Hold still, Zak!" I said. I started to brush him.

Now he was all ... Wiggly! Jiggly! Wobbly!

I was trying to brush him! It was hard. He had all these wrinkles! And he was all wiggling!

Then he flopped on the ground! He rolled on his back. He was scratching and rolling and flopping and panting and ...

Hey. I think this dog is ...

Ticklish!

Yes! Zack was scratching itches! Like he's all tickly. Kinda funny. But hard to groom!

Hm. The brush was too tickly. I picked up a blanket. I started rubbing him with it. And he goes ...

SIGH!

A happy noise. He stopped wriggling. He leaned on me. Then he ... moved on to my lap.

OOMPH! This Zak is short! But he weighs a TON!

"OK, I guess you like the blanket rub," I said. I rubbed him more. He sat on my lap. My leg was falling asleep. But I kept rubbing him! Making his fur all nice and shiny.

He was looking better! Then Zak climbed up on me and put his paws on my shoulders ... stuck out his tongue ... and gave me a big ... wet ... sloppy ... kiss!

Ack! I think his breath needs some ... um ... grooming, too. PU!

"Looks like you have a big fan, Maddy!" Eve walked back in. Zak was all over my lap. Getting all comfy and cozy. And drooly, too.

"Zak, I think you have to get off now," I said, trying to move him from my lap. He wasn't budging!

"Zak doesn't take to everyone, you know," Eve said. "He must really like you."

Ohmigosh.

Then Zak goes, BURP!!

OK! Um! Can we remove this dog from my lap, now? Please?!

"Come on, Zak," Eve said. "You look gorgeous. Let's show you off to the other dogs in their cages."

I brushed all the Zak fur off me. And Zak goo and Zak dribble and drool and ooze.

I hope the next dog is ... more groomy!!!!

"I thought you might like to groom Buggie next," Eve said.

Yay! Buggie!

Eve brought over Buggie, wrapped in a blanket.

"Hello, little Buggie!" I said. Her white fur was still a little damp! She looked up at me with her big black eyes! But she was all shaky and shivery.

"Buggie's a little scared," Eve said. "She's been through a lot. And she still gets shaky. We have to be extra gentle with her."

"I'm just going to brush you," I told her. "Make you all nice and pretty." I held up my brush. Buggie started shaking.

I put the brush down. I started to pet her. Nice and slow. Buggie started to relax! OK! She wasn't shaking so much. I picked up the brush. And started to brush realllllllly slow. Really gently.

"Is that OK, Buggie?" I asked her.

"Werf!"

I think that was a yes! She was totally just lying there in my arms!

"You're such a little Snuggle Bug!" I told her.

Eve was talking to one of the guy volunteers. Then she got all upset. Then they both were all ... "Budget! Money! What are we going to do?"

I didn't mean to listen. But they were kinda loud.

I brushed her fur. She had a big floppy piece of hair in her face. I went over to my backpack. I took one of my little hair bands out. I put it in her fur.

AWWWW!!! A little puppytail!

"You look soooo cute, little Huggie Bug!" I told her.

"Oh how adorable!" Eve came over to where I was sitting.

"Buggie looks great! You've done a wonderful job, today."

"Thanks," I said. "Um, can I ask you a question?"

"Of course."

"I totally didn't mean to listen. But I heard you guys talking about running out of money?" I asked.

Eve sighed.

"Well, on one hand, things are going great. Too great almost. We haven't been open very long. And we have more dogs than we anticipated! Our budget is stretched."

"Will everything be OK?" I asked.

"We're going to make sure of that," Eve said. "But you see how much it takes to keep this place going. Dog food, dog toys, dog treats ... we're going through blankets so fast!"

Oh! That's so ... sad!

"We're going to try to get some publicity," Eve said. "Try to get our name out there to raise some funds. We're participating in a mall event next week."

"What are you doing?" I asked.

"There's a new pet supply store opening in the mall," Eve said. "We're going to have some information about our shelter there. About adopting dogs and how to donate to help."

The front door bell jingled.

"That's probably your Mom," Eve said. "It's time for you to go."

Already?

"I wish I could stay longer!" I said.

"I'm glad you're enjoying it here," Eve said. "We're enjoying having you."

I gave Buggie a little pat on the nose. And handed her back to Eve. I waved. Bye-bye, Buggie!

See you soon!

# chapter 8

Poor little doggies!

What if there's no money for blankets? I thought about all the dogs sleeping all comfy on their blankets. What if there's no money for toys? What will they play with? What if there's no money for food? The dogs will be so hungry!

I thought about:

- ★ Sparkle and Sunny! Ginger! Dotti!
- ★ What will Rocky do if he doesn't have toys to play with?
- ★ What will Buggie do without her snuggly blankets???

And what will all the dogs do if there's no dog shelter?!! What if they ran out of money and had to close down and then the dogs didn't have anywhere to stay!!!

Oh noooo! I was seriously worried!!! I needed to do something. But what could I do??!!

I couldn't stop thinking about it!

"Maddy! What are you thinking about?" Claire said.

"You're so quiet!" Kacey said.

"Something's wrong." That was Isabel.

I snapped back to reality! Here at Limited Too Headquarters. With the TOO Crew! We were waiting for Lauren. Today was the day we would be fit models.

Which was way exciting! Way cool! Awesome and excellent! Except ...

"OK," I said. "You're right. I'm worried. About the dogs!"

I just couldn't help it! I told them what Eve had said.

They were all ... Oh no! What if there's no food? No toys? No blankets? No shelter?!?!

"We have to do something!" Claire said.

"I know," I said. "But what? Eve did tell me they were doing something at the mall. Next week."

"We have to help!" Isabel said.

"Count me in," Kacey was all like Yeah!

"What do you think we can do?" asked Claire. Then Lauren walked in.

"Hi girls," Lauren said. "How are you today?"

"Not so great!" I burst out.

Lauren looked at us.

"What's the matter?" she asked. "What's wrong?"

"Maddy and I have been volunteering at this dog shelter," Claire told her. "And the shelter is having money problems."

"They don't have enough for food! Or toys! Or supplies!" Kacey said.

"We're going to help, though," Isabel said. "They're doing something at the mall next week. When the new pet store opens."

"I want to help! Those poor dogs!" I told her. "But I mean, what can I do?"

"I admire you want to help out," Lauren said. "Let's see if we can brainstorm some ideas. We have a store at that mall. Maybe we can help out a little. I'll call the pet center and see what they have planned."

"Thanks, Lauren," I said. "You really think I could help?"

"I think we could all help!" Kacey said.

"I'm in," said Isabel.

"We should call Eve and ask her what we could do," Claire said.

Yeah! OK! Yay!

"I have extra minutes left on my cell phone," Claire said. "Do you want to call now?"

Claire dialed the number and handed it to me.

When Eve got on the phone I told her! I was worrying about the shelter! And that the TOO Crew wanted to help! What could we do? Anything at all?

And Eve said ...

Yes! We could help. We could help out at the mall event. This is what Eve told me:

- **The dog shelter is going to have a table set up at the mall by the new pet store.**
- **We would bring in some dogs.**
- **We could sit at one of the tables asking for dog food, toys, blankets and other donations.**

And Eve said we could make some flyers to pass around so people would know about it.

I told Kacey, Isabel, and Claire and they said ... YES! They would help!

I was feeling way better now. Now, it was time to ... FIT MODEL!!!!

But wait. OK, I was kinda nervous! I mean, I wanted to do it right!

"Um, Lauren," I asked. "Can I ask one more question. How can I be a good fit model?"

"Relax, Maddy," Lauren said. "You'll be fine. It's good to be relaxed and comfortable when you're trying on the garments. This is what you'll do:

- ★ We'll try on clothes for one of the departments. Like the pants department. Or the skirt department. Or coat department. Whichever department is the priority that day.
- ★ There will be people there to see how the clothes look and how they fit.
- ★ They'll ask us our opinion about the clothes.

"Our opinion?" Isabel said. "Like if we like the clothes or not?"

"Yes. And also if you think they're comfortable. If they fit right. If they're styles you'd wear at school and at home."

"That's so cool!" Kacey said. She jumped up and high-fived us!

"This is so perfect for Isabel," Claire said. "She knows how to style!"

"Thanks, Claire," Isabel said. "I gotta say this! I'm way psyched to see the styles!"

I was, too! Still kinda nervous! But excited!

One of the women came out. And called.

"Maddy! Fit room #3!"

That's me! Here I go! Maddy the Fit Model!

There were three women in the room. They introduced themselves. There was a:

★ **Buyer:** She chooses the fashions that are appropriate for girls and for the season that the store will buy and carry.

★ **Designer:** She identifies the fashion trends for the season for styles and fabrics and trims.

★ **Tech designer:** She analyzes the fit, quality, and construction of the clothes.

"Hi Maddy," the tech designer said. "We have your measurements from the other day. Today we're going to have you try on some skirts."

OK! That's cool. I'm going to be a skirt fit model.

She took out some different skirts. Long! Short! Denim! Floaty! Flowery! Mod! She handed me a long blue and pink floaty skirt with flowers on it. I tried it on.

"It's meant to be a tiny bit shorter," said the designer.

"I'd say a quarter inch," said the tech, pinning it.

I stood really still.

"You have great posture," the tech said. "That's helpful when you stand up straight like that."

"That looks better," the buyer said. "Good fit."

"OK, Maddy, why don't you walk around a little," said the designer. "How does it feel?"

Um ... I wanted to say something smart! To be a good fit model!

"It feels ... floaty. I mean, actually it's really comfortable." It was really comfy. But ... it wasn't exactly something I would wear. I didn't want to say that, though. It might hurt their feelings!

"What do you think about the look?" the buyer asked.

OK! Um! Well!

"It's way pretty," I said. "I like the blue. Blue's my favorite color ..."

"But ... I can tell you're holding back," the designer said. "We really want your honest opinion. If you don't like it, that's fine! If it's not you, that's fine!"

"Oh! OK! Well, it's not really me. I don't wear floaty flower things," I said. "But you know what? Claire does! She's right outside!"

I whipped open the door. Isabel and Claire were out there waiting.

"Guys! What do you think of this skirt?" I asked.

"Totally Claire!" Isabel said. At the same time, Claire said, "I love it!"

I turned back.

"See? So you'll sell a lot of these to Claires!" I told them.

"Great!" the designer said. "That was certainly an honest opinion."

Next I tried on a mod skirt. They thought it should be longer! I did, too! But was it my style? Nope!

"Not me. Too much for me. But definitely Isabel!" I said. "The other girl out there! She would love it."

The next skirt was a skort. It fit perfectly!

"This one is soooo a Kacey," I said. "She only wears skirts if she has to! But it's comfy! And she'd wear this with sneakers in the summer!"

Then I tried on a denim skirt. I loved it!

"I love this!" I told them.

"Great," said the buyer. "So this would be your favorite."

YUP!

"That's very helpful, Maddy," the buyer said. "Thank you!"

I went out to the lobby. Isabel was waiting out there.

"Hey!" she said. "I just tried on the coolest pants. Wait til you see what styles are coming in! I can't wait to give Nicole and

Tia the scoopage!"

"One of those skirts in there was so you! I said. It's so funny how we all have our own styles!" I said. "But I'm not sure what my style is exactly. I mean, Kacey's sporty ... Isabel's trendy ... Claire's style is more pretty. So what am I?!!"

Isabel was about to say something. But then Kacey came out!

"Hi!" Kacey bounced out. "What'd you guys try on?"

We told her what we tried on.

"I tried on coats," she said. "All kinds of coats! Then I had to pick my fave. I liked this sporty looking one."

No big surprise! Kacey was super-SUPER-sporty!

"I'm in total shock here! I just got a sneak preview of what styles are coming!" Isabel said. "I got to tell them what I thought! I got to give MY opinion on fashion! How cool is THAT?!!!"

OK, how much does Isabel loooooooooove fashion?!!! Way so much! This job is perfect for her!

Fun for me. But like ... a dream come true for her!!!!!!!

My dream come true ... right now?

To help the dogs at the dog shelter!!!!!!!

Then Lauren came out.

"Maddy, I got some information about the pet store event," she said. "And I can help you help the dogs, too."

We were all YAY!

"The pet store is at the other end of the mall from our store," Lauren said. "So some of the shoppers might not be aware of what you're doing. So why don't you girls set up a table in front of our store? You'll be visible at both ends of the mall."

Great!

"That mall is pretty big!" Kacey said.

"We should make flyers or signs something," I said. "To pass around the mall."

"How about I get permission to do so," said Lauren. "You girls work with the shelter to make the flyers and signs."

"Thanks, Lauren," Claire said. "This is so nice of you!"

"It's a thanks for all your hard work," Lauren said. "And we're happy to support a good cause."

"Let's make a plan," Isabel said. "We need to make signs and flyers, right?"

"I can do them on my computer!" I said.

"I'll get copies printed out," Claire said.

"How about Kacey post the flyers around?" Isabel said. "You can ask Eve where she thinks they should go."

"Yeah! And I'll be there at the mall to help for sure!" Kacey said.

"Me, too," Isabel said.

Go, TOO Crew, go!

# chapter 9

From: MaddyBlue
Send to: DogShelterEve

Thanks for letting me stop by to take pictures of the dogs! Maddy

From: DogShelterEve
Send To: MaddyBlue

Anytime! Eve

So I was at my house. On the computer. My Dad was helping. He's really good at computers. We're making flyers! And signs! For the dog shelter!

And I had this idea.

Every time I see the doggies, I'm thinking, awww CUTE!!!!!!!

So I was thinking if people see the pictures, too, maybe they'll think that! And then they'll read about how the doggies need help! And they'll want to help out!

"Let's look at all the pictures," Dad said. "And we can pick which ones will work best."

I looked at pictures I'd taken at the shelter the day before. I love taking pictures. I'm not that great or anything. But once I even won a prize in a kid's photo contest! And OK, these turned out pretty good!

There was a photo of Rocky playing ball! And Ginger lying down. And Jake jumping in the air. Dotti looked all happy. Sparkle and Sunny looked all snuggly. And there was a picture of Buggie! A close-up. With her big huge black eyes. Her white fur fluffing around.

"Awwwww! That is so adorable!" My Mom came over and looked at the screen. "Who is that?"

"That's Buggie!" I told her.

"That is so adorable," my Mom said.

"Well, that's the response you wanted Maddy," my Dad said. "You've captured the viewer's attention! Let's start with that one."

I clicked to put the picture on a document.

Awwww ... it was the cutest little Buggie face. Looking like, "Help me! I'm so cute!"

"OK, now I need words," I said. "Like how we want people to donate. What we need and all that."

"That's right," said my Dad. "But you might also want a slogan. Something catchy. Like Donate for Dogs! Something to appeal to their emotions! Make them want to help!"

My Dad works in advertising. He knows this stuff.

Um ... I looked at the picture of Buggie.

I had an idea. This is what I wrote.

# Blankets for Buggie!

Buggie is one of the dogs available for adoption at the new Dog Shelter! She was found in the snow! She stays warm now at the shelter sleeping on her favorite blue blanket! She and other dogs are waiting for loving families to adopt them.

## Can't adopt a dog?

You can still help! The shelter desperately needs:

Dog food    Dog toys    Dog blankets    Donations

Then I left a space for the info about the Pet Store opening at the mall.

Then I made some other flyers with the other dogs on them:

## Food for Fifi!

## Toys for Theo!

## Dog Treats for Dotti!

"Maddy, that looks great!" Dad said. "Very persuasive."

Yay!

We e-mailed the file to Claire. She was going to get them printed. Isabel and Kacey would post them around.

The phone rang. I picked it up.

"Is Zack there?" It was a girl!

"Zackkkkkky! A girl for youuuuu!" I said.

Zack yelled from upstairs. "Sorry! Not home!"

"He isn't available at the moment," I said. "May I take a message?"

"Um, tell him Kylie called," the girl said. "No wait! Don't tell him! No, tell him. No, don't. OK, thanks! Bye!"

Click! She hung up.

I went upstairs. I knocked on Zack's door.

"I have a message for you," I said. "Kylie did not call."

"Huh?" Zack said. He stuck his head out the door.

"Well, that's what the message was," I said. "Kinda."

"Was it Kylie?" Zack said. He was all red! All blushy!

"You like Kylie!" I said.

"No way!" Zack said. "Yuk! Gross! Augh!"

"You like her!" I said. "That's why you're getting all this good behavior stuff! You want to impress her!"

"Yipes!" Zack said.

Slam! He closed the door.

Hee.

From: MaddyBlue
Send To: ClaireBear
Subject: Dog Shelter

Here's the flyer I made! Thx 4 copying it!

---

From: ClaireBear
Send To: MaddyBlue
Subject: Dog Shelter

I made copies. Bruno is taking me 2 give them 2
Isabel and Kacey 2day! They r going to post them
near the mall!

---

From: MaddyBlue
Send To: ClaireBear, SpaceyKacey, MizIs

thx!!!! cu at the mall!!!

---

From: DogShelterEve
Send To: MaddyBlue, ClaireBear, SpaceyKacey, MizIs

We will supply shirts and hats for the day. you
can wear with jeans!

# chapter 10

**PROJECT POOCH** at the Mall!

Check out my hat! I'm wearing an official volunteer hat
Eve gave me for the Pet Supply Store opening!
I'm at the mall! The mall's going to open in
half an hour! And here's the plan!

Eve and the volunteers at the dog shelter set up a table by the
new pet store. There would be another station at the other
end of the mall. In front of the Limited Too store.

The TOO Crew would be at that table. We would tell people
walking by about the shelter.

Eve came down to show me the table. She gave me a walkie-
talkie, too. She had the other one. In case we needed her!

"Hi Maddy!" Kacey and Isabel and Claire were here! They had
their hats on, too!

The TOO Crew was all here!

"We're here to give some serious help to those dogs!" Isabel said.

"Eve said she'd be down in a minute," I told her.

YEAH!

"Hi, TOO Crew!" Lauren was here!

"Hi, Lauren!" We said.

"We thought we'd supply some shirts for you," Lauren said. "To help out. And also as a thank you for fit modeling the other day."

She handed us each a bag. COOL!

"Well, we know they'll fit, right?" Isabel said. "Since you guys know what size we wear!"

"The ladies' room is over there," Lauren said. "And if you get locked in ..."

Ack! We were CRACKING up. Because of course ... we met when we were locked in a bathroom! At another mall!

"Claire, do you have your cell phone charged?" Kacey was laughing.

"Check!" Claire said.

"Maddy, do you have the walkie-talkie?" Kacey asked.

"Check!" I said.

"OK, we're prepared!" Kacey said. "Let's go!"

We all ran over to the bathroom.

I pulled out my t-shirt. It was light blue with a long-sleeved white T under it. And it had a cartoon puppy on it!

"Awww, my shirt is soooo cute!" I said. And my necklace with the dangly dog? Matched perfectly!

Kacey had a red and navy shirt with a cartoon dog dancing around on it! Isabel had an orange shirt with a dog's face on it. And Claire had a pink shirt with a kitten and a puppy on it!

"These are so perfect!" Kacey squealed.

"Let's go help the doggies!!!" I said.

"Food for Fifi!" said Isabel.

"Toys for Theo!" said Kacey.

"Dog treat for Dotti!" said Claire.

"Blankets for Buggie!" I said!

"FOR PROJECT POOCH!!!" We all yelled it together!!!!!! WOO HOO!!!!

We went out to our table. It had a jar on it and some brochures.

Claire had made big copies of the flyers. We sat down in the chairs behind the tables.

"These pictures are great," Isabel said, looking at the posters. "Look at those dogs!"

"Do you know how Buggie's doing?" Claire asked. "She's sooo sweet."

"She's good!" I said. "She has to take puppy medicine and she's still really tiny. But Eve says she's going to be fine."

Then these workers from Limited Too came out to say hi and wish us luck.

"We'll be sure to let people know you're out here," they told us.

People started walking around the mall. We were like, "Hi! Hi!" Then two people stopped.

"Hi, what's this all about?" a man and a woman said.

Eve had told us how to answer questions from people. I hoped I would do a good job!

"We're trying to raise awareness about a new dog shelter," I said. "And we're hoping to get donations to help the shelter continue its work."

"Well, that sounds like a worthy cause," the man said. "I'll take a brochure."

Then the woman gave us some money! She put it in the jar.

Woo hoo!

"Our first donation!" I said.

"Hi!" Some girls walking into Limited Too stopped at the table.

"Awww, cute doggies!" they said.

"I want to get the dogs a doggie toy," the girl said. "Can I buy them one?"

We told them where the pet store was. They said they would go up there later and drop off a toy at Eve's table.

Some people walked by. We'd be like "Hi! Hi!" But they were kinda going by fast.

"Hi Maddy!" It was Jordan, Petie and Sara! Some girls from my school. I'd told them I'd be here. But I didn't know they'd come!

And their arms were full of blankets!!!

"Wow, you guys," I said. That's so awesome.

"Our parents totally went through the closets," Jordan said.

"That's my blanket from when I was little," Petie said, holding out a pink one. "I thought one of the dogs could sleep on it now!"

"Sara, I thought you don't even like dogs that much!" I said.

"Well, yeah," Sara said. "I'm a cat person. But I can't let little dogs get all cold! I had to bring some blankets!"

"Thanks, you guys!" I said. That was way nice!

"Hi, honey! Hi girls," My family was here!

"How are things going?" Dad said. "The flyers look great.

"Pretty good," I said, looking around. "But, a lot of people are walking by us."

"I'll help!" Zack said. He took a bunch of flyers. "C'mon, Ma! Dad! Let's go hand out flyers."

Zack took off. We saw him walk up to this woman with a little boy in a stroller.

"Hello, ma'am!" he said. "You look like a caring person. Well, we're helping a volunteer dog shelter today. I bet your little boy would like a new dog! Or if not, you could help! With a donation!"

"Ohmigosh," I said. "My brother is so totally nutso."

Then the woman came over! And made a donation!

"But you have to admit ... he's doing a good job!" Isabel said.

My parents waved at me. And followed Zack who was talking to a guy with a baby.

Then this girl with long brown hair came over. She was carrying a bag of dog food. And then she said, "Hi, Claire!"

"Oh! Hello! This is Hannah," Claire said politely. "These are my friends Maddy, Kacey, and Isabel."

"Hi," Hannah said.

"Thanks for the dog food," Isabel said.

"Claire told me about this at horseback riding," Hannah said. "And I wanted to help."

I bet this was the girl Claire told me about. The girl she wanted to get to know at horseback riding lessons! But she was so shy ...

"Thanks, Hannah," Claire said.

"Well, OK," the girl said. "Bye."

"Wait!" I said. "You like horses? Have you seen Claire's horse yet? Skydancer?" I asked Hannah.

"No," Hannah said.

"Skydancer's so pretty! Maybe you could go see her sometime!" I said. I looked at Claire.

"Yes!" Claire said. "I mean ... maybe you could come over to my house sometime? Like after lessons next weekend."

"That would be cool!" Hannah said. She looked all surprised ... but happy. "I'll ask!"

They said good-bye!

"Thanks, Maddy," Claire whispered to me.

I remembered when I first met Claire. She was so ... glamorous looking! So pretty! I thought she was stuck up! I almost didn't want to talk to her. But then I found out she was just shy!

"That was nice that your friend came," Kacey said.

"And yeah!" Isabel said. "That reminds me. My friends Nicole and Tia went around school. And collected for our donation, too." She put an envelope in the jar.

We waited. Some people went into the stores. But didn't stop by. We were like, "Hi!" They said, "Hi!" But kept going.

"If you could adopt one of these dogs, which would you choose?" Kacey asked.

"It's hard," Claire said. "I guess since I have two big dogs, I'd want a small dog. I like Fifi. She's so little and fluffy. Or one of those puppies, Sunny or Sparkle."

"That Dalmation looks mod. All black and white," Isabel said. "I'd probably choose Dotti."

"I like this one. Jumping! Catching a ball! He looks like he's all bouncy!" Kacey said. All bouncing around, just like Rocky! "I'd choose Rocky!"

"Are you talking about ... this Rocky?!!" There was Rocky on a leash! This guy in a DOG SHELTER VOLUNTEER hat came over to us. He was walking Rocky! I recognized him from last time I was at the shelter.

"Hey, I'm Tim," he said. "Eve thought you might like a little company. So I brought Rocky down to visit."

"Hi Rocky!" Claire and I said. He was jumping all around. All bouncy! So excited to see us!

We all were petting him. He was jumping all over us! "Arf!

Arf!"

"Well, hello little fella!" A man stopped to see Rocky. Rocky was so excited. Running around. "Arf! Arf!" The man put a donation in the jar and took a brochure. Then three girls were all, Awww! He's so cute! They took a brochure, too.

Tim gave me the leash. I started to walk Rocky around. But Rocky didn't want to walk! He wanted to run and jump! He jumped on the ledge of the fountain! He jumped on my chair! He was jumping and bouncing all over!

People were stopping to watch Rocky.

"Rocky gets some serious attention!" Isabel said. "He's a good fundraiser!"

That gave me an idea. If one dog was getting a lot of attention ...

"Are there any other dogs here?" I asked Tim.

"Yes, we brought some of the friendliest ones," Tim said.

I told him my idea. And then I buzzed Eve on the walkie-talkie. And we made a plan.

# chapter 11

"Announcing the first ever DOG SHELTER TALENT SHOW!" Zack was saying as he passed out the flyers. "Fifteen minutes! You won't believe your eyes!"

Yes! We were going to put on a mini-talent show! To get people to stop! To watch the dogs! And help out the shelter! We hoped.

Like that TV show I saw, *Dog Stars!*

I wanted to get more people over here. So I thought of a talent show. Kacey and Isabel and Claire were all YEAH! Eve was all, sounds fun!

But eek! Yikes! Would the dogs show their talents?

"Your brother's really helpful!" Claire said.

"Putting his mouth to good use for a change," I told her. "But actually, well, I have to admit. He's been kinda good lately."

No sneaking ketchup into my chocolate milk! No making weird noises when I was on the phone with my friends! No drawing mustaches on my face when I was sleeping!

I had been ... free of Zack-age for two weeks!!!

I didn't know how much longer THAT would last.

But I'd like it while it lasted! My parents were watching Zack tell people about the talent show. They were smiling. They were liking this new and improved Zack, too!

Eve and the volunteers came down with the dogs.

"Nice shirts!" Eve said to us. We were like, "Hi Eve! Hiii Dogs!"

People started to stop! Girls came out of Limited Too! We were getting a crowd! Everyone was looking at the dogs!

Isabel was going to be the emcee. She stood up and said ...

"Presenting the Talented Dogs of the New Dog Shelter! First up is ... Jake the Frisbee Champ!"

I had remembered what Jake had wanted to play when I was volunteering. Frisbee! I'd also remembered how I tossed the frisbee. And, um, almost knocked Eve out! Sooo ....

Kacey was going to throw the frisbee! She had an awesome arm!

She tossed Jake his frisbee. He jumped and caught it in his mouth!

Everyone clapped. Then Kacey tossed it way high and he

caught it again! Then she flung it from behind her back ... and yes! Jake caught it again! Everyone clapped again!

"That was Jake, and remember he's available for adoption!" Isabel said. "Next up is ... Fifi the Dancing Dog!"

Lauren gave us a thumbs up. And the music from the Limited Too store cranked up so we could hear it.

Claire brought Fifi out. She held a treat over Fifi's head. And Fifi got up on her hind legs and started dancing! Her little paws were waving in the air!

Everyone was like Ohhh! Look at the cute dancing dog!

Claire fed Fifi the treat. And the audience clapped.

"Look, more people are watching," Claire whispered after Tim took Fifi off.

"The dogs at the dog shelter are very well-behaved. Some of them are even very well-trained," Isabel announced.

And to show this off would be ... Dotti!

Claire brought Dotti out.

"Shake," Claire commanded. And Dotti did it! Everyone clapped. Then Claire told Dotti to sit. And Dotti did. And to roll over. And she did.

"Where's Dotti?" Claire asked.

Dotti put her doggie paws over her eyes. And played Peek a Boo!

"Wow!" I said. "Claire really is good with Dotti!"

"Now wave good bye!" Claire told Dotti. And Dotti held up her paw. And waved good bye at the audience.

Everyone clapped for Dotti!

"Now before the next act, we need to show you how cute these dogs are at the dog shelter," Isabel said. "Look at these puppies, Sammy and Sparkle. Sooooo cute, right?"

She held up the two puppies. She'd put purple bows on their heads.

The crowd was like Awwwwwwwwww. Cute!

"And now, the next performer is ..." Isabel said. She looked around. Tim brought over ... ZAK! That crazy dog, Zak! Tim gave me Zak's leash.

Isabel looked at me.

Ohmigosh. We had nothing prepared for Zak! I knew Jake could frisbee! And Fifi could dance! And Dotti obeyed commands. And the puppies couldn't do anything but they looked so cute. SO ... I was like ... uh ... uh ... what should we do?

"This is Zak!" I said.

I walked Zak out. And the crowd went, Ohhhh! Because Zak is so ... interesting looking.

And then all of a sudden, Zak went, Ohhhh, too! Sort of howling. But also he kind of began, well ... singing. Then he went AAAOOOOWW! Yup. Like he was singing.

"Is that dog yodeling?" I heard my father ask.

"Presenting Zak the, er, singing dog!" Isabel said.

And then Zak went AAOOOOAHHH! OOOOahhhhH!

Everyone clapped for the singing dog. And then Zak stopped singing. And went BURP!

Everyone started CRACKING up.

"A comedian dog," somebody said. "Very funny."

"That dog ROCKS!" my brother yelled out. Figures!

I dragged Zak off the stage. I didn't know what noise that dog would make next!!!

"And now for our grand finale. We present ... Rocky on the Amazing Mall Dogstacle Course!"

Kacey ran out with Rocky on a leash. We'd set up an obstacle course in the mall.

"First, the high jump!" Isabel said.

Rocky jumped over a chair! And then right over one of the mall benches!

Everyone clapped.

"Now, Rocky will demonstrate great balance on a balance beam!" Rocky ran along the ledge of the fountain. Go, Rocky, go!

But then ... stop Rocky, stop?

Rocky stopped! He stuck his head in the fountain! He was drinking from the fountain! Slurp! Whoops!

"Our contestant needs a water break!" Isabel said. We were CRACKING up!

"And now, for the most difficult part," Isabel said.

"Jumping through hoops! Yes, Rocky will jump through the hoops, generously provided by the toy store right over there!"

Rocky jumped through a hoop Claire was holding. Then a higher one! Then ... I was holding a way, way, high up one! I was holding my breath! Could Rocky do it!!!

Rocky did it!!! Woo hoo!!!!

The crowd started chanting! They were like, ROCKY! ROCKY! ROCKY!!!!

Kacey gave Rocky some extra treats for that!

"Good boy, Rocky," I said, patting his head.

Then it was my turn to talk! OK! A little nervous. But I'd do it! For the doggies!

"We hope you enjoyed the show," I said. "I'm a volunteer with the dog shelter. All of these dogs you see are available for adoption. Also, please take a brochure and read about the ways you can donate toys, dog food, blankets or money! OK? OK! Thanks!"

I jumped down.

"That was wonderful" Eve called out to me.

Then all of these people started coming over asking about the shelter!

Taking brochures!

Donating money in the jar!!!

"Excuse me," this woman and man came over with a little girl in a stroller. "May we meet Fifi?"

Eve brought Fifi over to her. They started talking.

"I have to see the Dogstacle course dog," this man was saying to Tim. He brought Rocky over on the leash. Rocky was all "Hi! Hi!" Bouncing up and down!

The man started talking to Tim. And petting Rocky.

Kacey, Isabel, Claire and I were busy, too! Passing out flyers! And brochures!

A woman came out of the Limited Too store with her daughter.

"Look at that picture!" the girl said. "That is the cutest dog ever!"

They came over and looked at the posters.

"That's Buggie," I said.

"Is she available for adoption?" the woman asked.

"I've been wanting a dog for soooo long!" said the girl. "My parents finally said yes!"

"Well, she was sick," I said. "So you have to ask Eve."

Eve came over. She told them Buggie should be ready to adopt later in the week!

Ohmigosh! Buggie! She was going to get adopted! I would miss her sooo much!

"We'll come in to the shelter this week," the woman said. "And bring home a puppy!"

"We'll look forward to seeing you!" Eve said.

Looks like Buggie would be adopted. I hoped I'd get a chance to say goodbye to Buggie first.

The people started leaving.

"Whoa!" Kacey said. "Check out the money jar! I mean, some people even wrote checks!"

"Some people said they were going upstairs to the new pet store," Isabel told Eve. "They're going to buy supplies! And drop them at your table up there!"

"I guess I better get upstairs to meet those people," Eve said. "This really went well. Thanks again, girls."

Lauren came out of the store.

"Hi, girls," she said. "Looks like that was a big success."

"Yeah!" we all said.

"You guys always put your all into things. That's one of the reasons we want you to do special TOO Crew assignments. Speaking of which, while I've got you here would you like to know your next assignment?"

Kacey, Isabel, Claire and I all went, "YEAH!"

What would we be doing?!?!?!?!?

"We'd like you to go on a buying trip. Which is a trip where we check out fashions and trends. And buy items we'll sell in the stores in the future. This particular buying trip will be in ... New York City."

NEW YORK CITY! Ohmigosh! We were all like WHOA!!!!!!

"New York?! I always wanted to go there!" Kacey said.

"You'll love it," Claire said. "It's one of my favorite places in the world."

We looked at Isabel. She looked practically in shock!

"A buying trip? Me on a fashion buying trip?" Isabel said. Oh yeah! This was a dream trip for her! She wants to be a fashion designer. This would be perfect for her!

And how cool would this be in NEW YORK CITY!!!

COOLEST OF COOL!!!!!!!!

"I'll take that as a yes," Lauren said. "Details to come."

# chapter 12

## PROJECT POOCH Day #6

My Mom was dropping me off at the dog shelter. For my last regular volunteer day. I had volunteered six times. My school project was over! This was supposed to be my last day. I would write an essay about it for homework. Then I was supposed to be done.

Danielle had said goodbye to the library. Jordan had said goodbye to people at the senior citizens home. Sara and Petie had said goodbye to the kids they were tutoring.

But ... it wasn't going to be my last day. I'd asked Eve. And she said yes. I was officially going to be a once-a-month dog shelter volunteer! I'd be back!

So I wouldn't have to say goodbye to the dogs!!!!!!!!

I did have to say goodbye to the New Improved Zack though. Because last night the phone rang.

"Is Zack there?" this girl said.

"Who's calling please?" I asked.

"Um, Stephanie," she said.

"Zackie, a girl for youuuuu!" I said. But not too teasing. I mean, he was super helpful at the mall and everything.

I heard Zack pick up. A couple seconds later I heard something go ... STOMP! STOMP! STOMP! STOMP!

Zack stomping down the stairs.

"How's your girlfriend?" I asked him.

"No girlfriend," Zack said. "No girls EVER!"

But he looked ... bumming.

"What happened?" I asked him

"Stephanie said that Kylie changed her mind and now likes Carter, that's all. OK? OK!" Zack went to the fridge. He got a can of soda out.

"Oh," I said. "That's a bummer."

"Whatever," Zack said. He stood there drinking a soda. He looked sad.

I went into the family room and picked up my book I was reading. I started reading about this girl and her friends. This book was way funny. I was laughing. But then I stopped.

Zack walked by. He still looked super saddy sad.

"Sorry about the girl," I said.

"Whatever," he said. "Do you want this soda? I changed my mind."

"Sure," I said. I popped open the top.

SPLLLOOOOOOOOOOSH!!!!!!!

Ack! The soda exploded all over me! Pouring out the top and all over me! Sticky wet soppy soda!!!

"Zack!" I yelled. "You shook that can up! You exploded me on purpose!!!"

"Ha!" Zack said. "Gotcha!"

I jumped over the couch! Chased after him!

"Yipes!!!" Zack bolted up the stairs. Way fast.

Argh!

So anyway. The Evil Zack was back!!!

And I was back at the dog shelter!!! I walked inside.

"Hi Eve!" I said. "Thanks for letting me come back! Even though my school project is over."

"Are you kidding? We're thrilled to have you," she said.

"I just couldn't stand it if I had to say goodbye to the doggies forever! I mean, Rocky? Ginger? Fifi? The puppies? Buggie? I would miss them so way much!"

"Well, remember Maddy," Eve said. "As much as you bond with the dogs, you don't want to get too attached to any one. Our goal is to get our dogs adopted."

"I know," I sighed. It was hard to say goodbye! But she was right!

"And we have the TOO Crew to thank for our most recent adoptions!" Eve said. "Let's take a walk to the kennels and I'll fill you in."

We walked to the dogs.

"Hi, Dotti!" I said. She came over and licked me. I went over to see Rocky. But it wasn't Rocky in the cage! There was a big tan dog sleeping in there. The sign on the cage said "Queenie."

"Do you remember the man who asked about Rocky at the

mall?" Eve asked. "He came in the next day and took him home. Now we have Queenie."

Oh, yay! Yay for Rocky! But it still was kinda weird.

I went over to Fifi's cage. Except it wasn't Fifi! It was a black and white dog with floppy ears.

"That's Kramer," Eve said. "He's a Springer Spaniel mix."

Oh! Fifi was gone, too! I thought about the time I had groomed her! How she loved to be fluffed! And petted! And how she danced!! Bye, bye Fifi.

Then Kramer said, "Arf!" He came over, with his tail wagging. He stuck his nose through the bars.

Awww! He's a sweetie!

"It's sad to see your favorites go," Eve said. "But there are always more dogs coming in!"

"Who else is gone?" I asked. I didn't want any more surprises!

"Well, the puppies Sammy and Sparkle were also adopted thanks to your talent show," Eve said.

ZWAK! ZWAK!

Well, Zak was still here!

But I really most wanted to know about Buggie.

"Those were the four adoptions this week," Eve said.

I went over to Buggie's cage!

"Hi cute little Buggie!" I said to her. She came over to me. "Hi little Lovie Bug!"

"Yes," Buggie is still here," Eve said. "She hasn't gone yet."

But then I saw it. A sign on her cage. It said, Reserved for Adoption. And it had today's date.

"What does that mean?" I asked Eve.

"Well, that means that Buggie is able to be released today," Eve said. "She is well enough and old enough to be adopted. And somebody who met the requirements has requested her today."

Oh! Buggie was being adopted! By the Mom and daughter that were at the mall, I guess.

I know. I know. I should be so happy for her! But I'll miss little Buggie!!!! At least I'll get to say goodbye.

"May I hold her?" I asked Eve.

"I'll give you some time to visit, I promise" Eve said. "But first, there's a surprise waiting for you in the break room."

She pointed to the break room. So we went in and ...

There were balloons! And Tim the volunteer was there. And ...

"MADDY!!!!!!!!"

CLAIRE was there! And Kacey??!! And Isabel??!! The whole TOO Crew was there!

HUH??

"I wanted to thank you for your help at the mall!" Eve said. "So we're having a pizza party for the TOO Crew!"

OK ... YAY!!! And YUM!!!

I sat down between Kacey and Claire! Eve passed out plates.

"Half of it is extra cheese and pepperoni especially for you Maddy," Claire said.

That's my fave!

"What great donations we got from the mall," Eve said. "And

look at all the dogs in your Dog Talent Show that were adopted! We might have to make that a regular event!"

I was so smiling!!!!!!!

"So when Eve invited us over we were psyched to come see this place," Isabel said. "You and Claire have to show us around after we eat! Kacey and I want to see the dogs!"

"Sure," I said.

"Fifi, Sammy, Sparkle and Rocky got adopted," I told them. "How awesome was Rocky on that obstacle course?"

"And how way cute was Fifi dancing?" Kacey said.

"Maddy, that was so cool how you knew what each dog could do," Isabel said. "And then we got to show it off!"

"Maddy's a natural with the dogs," Claire said.

Awwww!

"Claire is great, too!" I said.

But Claire goes, "I love them, but you have this connection with the dogs!"

Yeah! I kinda feel like I do!

"Why don't you show the girls around, now?" Eve said.

We went back to the kennel. I introduced them to Ginger and Max and Kramer.

Isabel and Kacey were like, Awwww! Cuute!

Then we all said hi to Dotti and Jake and Queenie.

"Hey, there's the burping dog!" Kacey said.

Yup, and there was Zak. He was going Zwak! Zwak!

But I saw that Buggie wasn't in her cage. Then Eve came out carrying her in a blanket.

"We just had Buggie checked and groomed," Eve said. "Remember, she's going home later today. Why don't you show her to your friends?"

Eve put Buggie in my arms. I held her out for everyone to see.

"Oooooh! Awww!!" Kacey and Isabel and Claire were all petting her soft white fur.

"She is just way too cute," Kacey squealed.

"Maddy, why don't you spend a few minutes alone with Buggie," Eve suggested.

Claire took Kacey and Isabel up front.

I sat down and put Buggie in my lap.

"Hi Bugaboo," I said.

I thought about that time when I first saw her. She was all cold and shivery and scared. Cuddled up in a blanket!

But she let me hold her. Pet her. Brush her. She even let me put a little puppytail in her fur!

"Maddy!" Eve called. "Your Dad is here to pick you up!"

OH! I would have to say goodbye to little Buggie, soon. Sigh!

I went out front. My Dad and Zack were standing with Claire, Isabel, and Kacey.

"Hi Dad!" I said. "I didn't know you were coming!"

"This looks like a nice place you have here," Dad said to Eve. "Mind if I take a look around?"

"Me, too!" said Zack. "I wanna see some dogs!"

"Maddy can be your tour guide," Eve said. "She knows the ropes. Claire, Kacey, and Isabel would you mind waiting out front for a few minutes?"

So Eve and I took Dad and Zack around. Buggie fell asleep in my arms so I carried her with me. I showed them the grooming area. The dog runs outside. The kennels.

Zack was looking at all the dogs. And I guess ... talking to them.

"Woof!" he was saying to Max. "Rowf! Ruff ruff!"

"Maddy seems to really enjoy coming here," Dad said.

"Oh, she's been very helpful. And Maddy really has a special connection with the dogs," Eve said. "She's very good with them."

Yay! I loved to hear that!

"Eve!" Tim was calling out. "Buggie's ready to be adopted! I need to get her ready."

Oh ... time to say bye to Buggie!

"You're a good dog, little Buggie," I said. I gave her a little kiss on her wet nose. I knew I had to say goodbye to the dogs! I was happy they could go to good homes! But it was hard!!! Especially little Buggie!

I carried Buggie out front. I handed her over to Tim. Tim took her into the back to get her ready.

Claire and Isabel and Kacey were looking at me like, Oh! Maddy will miss Buggie! So sad!

"Where's Buggie's new owner?" I asked. I looked around for the mother and the daughter from the mall.

"Actually, she's right here," Eve said. "That is, if you're interested."

OK, huh?

"The new owner is you, Maddy," Eve said. "If you want her, Buggie is yours. Yours to keep."

I looked at my Dad. Because he always says, NO DOGS, NO WAY! No way, no how and just plain NO!

"I know I've always said no," Dad said. "But, I've seen it for myself. How responsible you've been with the dogs. How much dogs mean to you. So go ahead, ask me."

"Uh ... Dad? May I have a dog?" I asked, all shaky-like.

And my Dad said ...

"YES!"

My Dad said yes? Is this a dream? I could have a dog???

But he was nodding. The answer is YES!!!!!!!!!!! I CAN HAVE A DOG!!!

And wait? I could have Buggie? I didn't have to say goodbye to her? Little Buggie could be MY dog?!?!?!?

**OH.**

**MY.**

**GOSH!!!!!!!!!**

**AHHHHHHHHHHHHHHHHHHHH!!!!**

I threw my arms around Dad!!!! I gave him the biggest hug EVER!

"Thank you thank you thank you thank you!"

"Don't forget to thank your mother, too," Dad said. "She's been on your side the whole time!"

Then Kacey and Isabel and Claire came running into the room. They looked at me and went:

**AHHHHHHHHHHHHH!**

"Congratulations, Maddy!" Claire said. Everyone was all dancing around.

"You guys knew about this?" I said.

They were all like YES! Eve had told them before I'd arrived! They had to keep it a big secret!!!

"We were busting!" Kacey said. "Did you see how we pretended to look all sad when you were telling Buggie goodbye!"

"Wait!" I turned to Eve. "What about the mother and daughter who were coming in to look at Buggie?"

"Oh," she said. "I kind of steered them to Sammy and Sparkle first. That's where the puppies went! After your parents called to let me know you could have a dog, I kind of figured you would like Buggie yourself."

"Thanks, Eve!" I said. I gave her a hug, too!

AHHHHHHHHHHHHH!

Tim came out. He handed me ...

MY DOG!!!

MY DOG BUGGIE!

MINE MINE MINE MINE MINE!

Buggie looked at me with her big black eyes like ...

"I'm yours!!!"

I kissed her wet little nose.

"Now Maddy, I know you always wanted a dog named Princess," Dad said. "But Eve thought you'd really bonded with Buggie. You certainly could choose another dog if you prefer."

"Ohmigosh," I said. "No way! I want Buggie!!"

"Anyway, you could name her Princess Buggie," Kacey said, bouncing all around.

"You are a little princess," I said to my puppy. "Your official name can be Princess Lovebug. But of course, we'll call you Buggie!"

Buggie went, "Werf!"

"I think she likes that!" said Eve.

"We've got the supplies ready in the car," Dad said. "Now we just need to get Zack. Where's Zack?"

"He's back with the dogs," Tim said. "One of the volunteers is back there watching him.

Tim, Dad and I went to get Zack. Where was he? Oh!

Zack was in Zak's cage.

My brother Zack was lying on the dog bed. My brother was being all huggy with the dog.

"Check this out, Dad!" Zack said. "Remember this dog? From the talent show? This dog is rockin'"

"That dog? That dog sneezes and goos on everything," I said.

"Come on out, Zack," my Dad said. "That's a pretty cool looking dog, I agree. But it's time to go."

A cool looking dog? Zak? He was all wrinkly and shloppy! I mean, no offense to Zak but ... he's not exactly a cutie! Dad thought he was cool looking? Maybe it's a guy thing.

"But Dad," Zack said. "It's fate."

"What?" Dad and I were all huh?

"This dog's name is Zak. And I'm Zack. We're both good looking and talented and awesome. We're made for each other," Zack said.

A Zack and Zak lovefest! Yeek!

My Dad's cell rang.

"Hang on guys," he said. "It's your Mom. I want to tell her Maddy is the proud owner of a dog."

He started talking to my Mom. I heard him say, "Happy ... Buggie ... coming home!"

"Time to go. Come out of there now, Zack," I said.

"Awww, let me play with my Alter-Zak," Zack said. "Zack Junior. Zack, Dog Version."

Dad came back over.

"Well," Dad said. "I've got Mom on the phone and she says she can't wait to see Buggie at home. And, Zack she has a message for you, too. We've noticed how well you've behaved lately. Your good grades. Your good citizenship award. Your notes from the teacher ... the good ones. We're very proud of you. So we have decided, if we're getting one dog ... what the heck. We might as well get two."

HUH?!!!

"I can get this dog?!" Zack yelled. "I can get this coolest, awesome rockin' dog!"

"If you agree to take care of it," Dad said.

"Wait!" I said. "OK! Another dog is great! Let's go look at ALL the dogs. Any dog! Not this one! He's all the things you said you didn't want!"

He's gooey!

He's messy!

He chews things!

He ... looks kinda freaky!

"Um, did you tell Mom which dog Zack wants?" I asked. Maybe once I told her it was the Burping Dog she'd change her mind!!!

"Maddy, you chose your dog. We will let Zack choose his," Dad said. "Plus, that Zak dog is a guy's dog. Yup. Something about him is pretty cool ..."

Eve came in and Dad told her the news.

"Well, what a surprise! I'll draw up the papers!" Eve said.

Oh. My. Gosh. Stop them!

"Dad, we can't do this! Um, we can't have two Zacks in the house," I said. "One is enough! More than enough!"

"Good point," Dad said. "Zack, we'll have to change your dog's name."

I didn't mean just the name. Ack! Ack!

"OK!" Zack said. "Lemme think. Did you see that cage? Maybe I'll call him Barbarian, Dog of Total Chaos. Or Ooze, Dog of Major Slime-age!!!"

Argh! "Zak wrecks everything!"

"What, Maddy?" Zack said. "Did you say Zak wrecks everything?!

Oops! Did I say that out loud?

"Wrecks! I like it!" Zack said. "Wrecks, Dog of Destruction! That's it! I'll name him Wrecks!!!"

Just then Dad walked in.

"Rex?" Dad said. "That's a fine dog name for a fine dog, son. We'll call him Rex."

"Wrecks, Dog of Destruction!" Zack said. "Perfect!"

Argh! Quick, think about something else.

"Werf! Werf!" Buggie was waking up! Yes! I would just think about Buggie! Not about the ... other dog. I snuggled her close. My sweet little Buggie.

OK, plus I looked at Zack. I remembered how sad he had been last night. He had been pretty bummed about that girl not liking him. Now he was smiling. Hugging the Dog Who Used to Be Named Zak.

So, wow! Zack and I were both getting dogs. This was way huge.

And then the Dog Who Used to Be Named Zak went ...

BURRRP!

"Nice one!" Zack my brother said to the dog. "I can beat you." Then my brother burped.

I better get out of here. I went back up front!

"What's going on?" Claire asked. Isabel and Kacey were like, yeah, what's up?

"You are so not going to believe this. Zack's adopting Zak!" I said. "My brother is getting that sneezy gooey bulldog with a fang creature. ACK!"

"Breathe, Maddy," Isabel said. "Think good thoughts. Focus on Buggie."

I looked at Buggie. I started to smile ... Yay! Buggie!

"Your Dad filled out all the paperwork already," Eve said. "But we need the new official owner to sign this last certificate."

Eve handed me the form and a pen.

**_Pet Owner Certificate_**

I, Maddy Elizabeth Sparks.
promise to provide a loving and
caring home for my new dog,

_Princess Lovebug (BUGGIE!!!!)_

Signed, the Dog's Owner:

_Maddy Elizabeth Sparks_

Witnessed by:

_Claire Isabel Kacey_

**Happy Face Rating:**

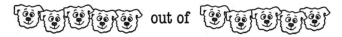 out of

# I HAVE A DOG!!!!!!!!!!!!!!!!!!!!!

The end ... but not for long!

'Cuz there's going to be more! So stay tuned!!!

**This Journal Belongs to:**

PRIVATE!  Maddy Elizabeth Sparks  KEEP OUT!!

So OK! Some people (like Brittany) thought that volunteering was going to be blah and boring and lame.

But ... no way! Volunteering was sooo awesome. Everyone said I really made a difference. Yes, me!!! I got to help all those cute little doggies!!! It felt soooo great!

So anyway. Before u go ... I have a question for u. Where would U want to volunteer someday?

☐ Help at a school! Helping younger kids learn to read and stuff!

☐ Helping older people at a senior home!

☐ Helping out at a library!

☐ Helping out at a hospital!

☐ Helping out at a nature place, like a park!

☐ Helping raise money for a good cause!

☐ Helping collect toys and food and stuff people need!

☐ Helping out a pet shelter (like me!!!)

☐ Other great ideas you have:

_____

_____

Kewl!

---

## ♡ YOUR DREAM DOGGIE ♡

What's YOUR dream doggie?! (write your answers below)

What kind of dog would it be?

What would you name your dog?

What would you nickname your dog?

What color would your dog be?

What color collar would your dog wear?

What tricks would your dog do?

OK!!! Bye! g2g! This is the end. But not really the end, of course! Because the TOO Crew has some WAY cool stuff coming up! Wait til you see what happens next!!!!

Be sure to look for Tuned In Episode #7! Coming exclusively to Limited TOO!

cu! ttyl!

xoxo Maddy

P.S. Hey? Guess what? There's some new book stuff coming out on LimitedToo.com. Sneak previews! Some new scoop! Seriously! Check it out!!!!!!!!